pos

The tap
an errie sou
tap tap. Tap: ta

A tree! It had

Was there a tre

Jane was not a g
she flung back the b
window and threw ope

'*Oh!*'

What she saw caused h   back, a hand
pressed to her mouth to stifle t   m that rose within
her. Bobbing up and down, at the level of the windowsill, were two faces. She could just make out the eyes,
and white teeth gleaming in the darkness . . .

JEAN URE

Faces at the Window

ƒCORGI
REEWAY

FACES AT THE WINDOW

A CORGI FREEWAY BOOK : 0 552 52790 4

First publication in Great Britain

PRINTING HISTORY
Corgi Freeway edition published 1994

Copyright © Jean Ure, 1994

The right of Jean Ure to be identified as the Author of
this work has been asserted in accordance with the
Copyright, Designs and Patents Act 1988

Set in Palatino by Kestrel Data, Exeter

Corgi Freeway Books are published by Transworld Publishers Ltd,
61–63 Uxbridge Road, Ealing, London W5 5SA,
in Australia by Transworld Publishers (Australia) Pty Ltd,
15–25 Helles Avenue, Moorebank, NSW2170,
and in New Zealand by Transworld Publishers (NZ) Ltd,
3 William Pickering Drive, Albany, Auckland.

Printed and bound in Great Britain by
Cox & Wyman Ltd, Reading, Berks.

FACES AT THE WINDOW

1

There was only one person at school who knew that Jane Lawlor's dad had had a big win on the pools and that was Lynn Freeman, because she was Jane's best friend. Lynn was sworn to deepest secrecy.

'Don't want begging letters, I suppose.'

'We've given lots to charity.' Jane was quick to make the point. Mum and Dad might have fought shy of publicity, but they'd been generous with their handouts.

'So how's it feel to be rich?'

'I wouldn't say we were rich exactly,' protested Jane. But they *were* rich, compared with what they had been before. Rich enough for her mum and dad to be talking of giving up work.

'And not a day too soon,' her dad had said. 'Be like to kill your mum, this had gone on much longer.'

By 'this', he meant the recession. Jane's dad was a builder with his own small business, working from home. Her mum did the books and looked after the correspondence – when there was any, which just lately there hadn't been. It seemed that people in London didn't have the money any more for loft conversions or patio extensions. The big pools win had come just in time.

'Another few months and I reckon we'd have gone under.'

Now Dad could stop worrying about Mum and her asthma, and Mum could stop worrying about Dad and his cholesterol, and for the first time in years they could afford a proper holiday.

'Florida,' said Jane. She screwed up her nose: Florida was naff. Jane had begged for Africa, or for Russia or China, but her mum wouldn't hear of it. Florida was what she had set her heart on.

'Disneyland,' said Lynn. 'Yuck!'

'Mum's never been abroad in her life before, except for day trips to France. Why she has to go and pick on Florida—'

' 'Cause she thinks it's classy. She thinks she'll meet the smart set. I suppose you'll go all snobby now.'

Jane looked at her friend, indignantly. There had been a note that was almost sneering in Lynn's voice.

'I will not!'

'I bet you will. New house, new school—'

'No-one's said anything about a new house or a new school!'

'You don't think they'll go on living in Shepherd's Bush?' said Lynn; and now there was definitely a sneer in her voice. 'Highgate or Hampstead—' she emphasized the Hs – 'that's where you'll end up. Living with the nobs.'

'I suppose they might move to a bigger house,' admitted Jane – surely that couldn't be called snobby? To move from a tiny terrace workman's cottage to a three-bedroom semi? – 'but they wouldn't ever leave this part of London. Not while my gran's still here.'

'They'll take your gran with them, dumbo! Give her a granny flat.' Lynn poured a whole ocean of scorn into the words *granny flat*. Granny flats were what the nobs had.

'My gran wouldn't move from the Bush.' Jane said it stoutly. 'She was born and bred here. And I'm not leaving Heathfield, whatever happens.'

Some people thought Heathfield High was a dump – Jane's parents did, as a matter of fact. There had been much wailing and beating of breasts in the Lawlor household when that was where Jane had been allocated – but she had been there five years now and felt a loyalty towards it. Next term she would be in the sixth form, working for her A levels; she aimed to be the first Heathfield pupil to get to university. And in any case, Lynn was there. She couldn't imagine school without Lynn.

'Even if they did move, I could still commute.'

'Take a bet?' said Lynn. 'Pound to a pinch of pig wotsit you'll end up at some posh place . . . jolly hockey sticks! Fraffly decent! Wah wah wah!'

'Honestly,' said Jane, 'I never knew you were so cynical!'

'I'm not cynical, ducky, I'm realistic. Guy wins a couple of million quid on the pools, he doesn't want to hang on in this dump.'

'It wasn't a couple of million,' muttered Jane; but it might just as well have been. After a certain number of noughts, when you weren't used to having money, you tended to lose count.

'So long as you don't start wearing fur and leather gear,' said Lynn. 'That really *would* be gross.'

'Yes, and you're gross for even suggesting it!' Jane aimed a swipe at her. She and Lynn were active members of the West London Animal Action Group, none of whom would be seen dead wearing animal skins. 'That's a calculated insult, that is!'

Lynn grinned. She knew perfectly well that Jane was as sound as she was.

'Don't forget the Boots demo Saturday.'

'I'll be there,' said Jane.

To begin with, having lots of money was undeniably fun. Mum stopped fretting, Dad relaxed, and Jane went on shopping sprees and bought all the clothes she'd always wanted but never been able to afford, such as a pair of Doc Martens made out of simulated leather, which cost very nearly as much as a pair of Doc Martens made out of real leather. Her mum looked at them and said wistfully, 'I do wish you'd wear something pretty sometimes,' but Jane preferred her Doc Martens and denims. You couldn't go on demos wearing something pretty. For one thing it wouldn't be practical (if, for instance, you had to run from the police) and, for another thing, it would make you look like some soft-line suburbanite from the Cats' Protection League who'd wandered in by mistake. (Not that Jane had anything against the Cats' Protection League, only that they weren't normally the sort of people you would expect to find on demos.)

'Such a shame,' sighed her mum, who had always hankered after seeing her in neat little dresses or frilly blouses and flowery skirts.

'You can't expect me to change my personality

just because we've suddenly come into the money,' said Jane.

'Not even one pretty dress?' pleaded her mum.

'Oh, Mum! For heaven's sake! Don't nag!'

In September, just before the start of the autumn term, they flew to Florida for ten days. Jane was determined to find everything vulgar and materialistic, and everything *was* vulgar and materialistic and she sent postcards to Lynn, telling her so; but all the same it was a lot more fun than Bournemouth.

The new term started and no-one would have guessed that Jane's dad was now a rich man. Mum was able to visit the hairdresser rather more often than she had used to, and even treated herself to what she called 'a facial' every now and again; and Dad took up golf, which was what he had always wanted to do, and bought himself a splendid new hi-fi system to play his old beloved records on; and once a week they all went out for a Chinese or Indian meal; but really and truly, apart from that, and nobody being worried any more whether work came in or whether it didn't – 'I reckon I've done my stint,' said Dad – things went on pretty much the same as before.

Lynn was wrong, thought Jane. Having money might remove some of the stress, but it didn't change your basic way of life. Just because you had a few hundred thousand in your bank account instead of an overdraft didn't mean you were suddenly going to go mad and start living it up.

Jane settled back, comfortably, to work for her A levels, campaign for animal rights and go on demos in her new Doc Martens. Situation normal: no change.

It came as a shock when one day at the start of

December her dad said, 'Well, then, Janey! How d'you fancy moving into the country?'

'Pardon?' said Jane.

'Moving into the country! How'd you fancy it?'

'You can't be serious?' said Jane.

'I am, girl! Never been more serious in my life.'

'Look.' Her mum held out a newspaper cutting. Jane took it, grudgingly.

'What's this?'

'Where we're thinking of going.'

'Bed and breakfast in an English country house?'

'It could be turned into a proper little guest house.' Her mum leaned over her, eagerly pointing at the picture.

'Shallaford Hall, East Sussex,' read Jane. *'Twelve miles Lewes. Good hunting country – Hunting* country?' She turned accusingly to her mum. *'Horses for hire for hunts or hacks?'*

'Yes, well, we wouldn't keep up that part of it, of course.' Her mum spoke hurriedly. 'It's the house we're interested in. Imagine! A lovely little guest house right in the heart of the country!'

'What do you want a guest house for? I thought the idea was that you were stopping work? I thought you'd retired!'

Her mum and dad exchanged glances. They had known they would have trouble with Jane.

'The fact is,' said her dad, 'not having any work to do is all very fine for a month or so but when you've been used to being busy – well! It gets a bit boring, quite honestly.'

'A bit aimless,' said Jane's mum.

'So, what we thought, something like this would be ideal.'

Jane stared at him in disbelief. Ideal? It would be grotesque! Buried in the country? Running a *guest* house? 'You'd hate it!' she said.

'Oh, no, I don't think so,' said her mum. Her mum was sounding really excited; like a child looking forward to Christmas.

'A load of strangers tramping about all over the place? Living cheek by jowl with you?'

'They wouldn't be living cheek by jowl. We'd have our own private quarters, the same as they have now.'

'Who has now?' Jane spoke sullenly. 'And why are they offloading it, anyway?'

'I suspect,' said Jane's dad, 'it's because they can't make a go of it.'

'So what makes you think you and Mum could?'

''Cause we've got our heads screwed on right, and we've got the capital to do something with the place.' Now Jane's dad was sounding excited as well. If there was one area of the building trade at which he had excelled, it was restoring old houses. He had always had a passion for them. 'It seems it's been let go a bit, but nothing that can't be put right.' Mr Lawlor leaned over and took the newspaper cutting from Jane. 'A perfect example, that is, of an early Victorian residence . . . good solid stuff. Built like a fortress. Nothing wrong with the basic fabric.'

'I think it looks hideous,' said Jane.

'Yes, well, you would, wouldn't you?'

Jane pointedly ignored her dad. She turned to her mum.

'If you really have to go and do something daft like running a guest house, why can't you do it in London?'

13

'We want to get out of London. For the sake of your mother's health.'

'Jane, you'll love it when you're there,' said her mum. 'I'm sure you will.'

'You haven't already gone and bought it?' cried Jane.

'Not yet; we're still thinking about it. We're going down tomorrow to have a look. You could come with us if you wanted.'

Her mum looked at her, hopefully. Jane tossed her head.

'I can't take time out of school! I'm working for exams. And even if *you* go and bury yourselves in the country, I'm not going to! I'm staying right here, where I belong.'

'I don't know how you'll do that,' said her dad, 'seeing as you won't have a roof over your head.'

'Neil! Don't be too hard on her. It's a new idea, give her time to get used to it.'

'I won't ever get used to it,' said Jane. 'I'll go and live with Lynn, if necessary. And what about Gran? How's she going to feel, left on her own?'

'She won't be left on her own, she'll come with us.'

'She won't like that,' said Jane. 'Gran's independent. She wouldn't want to live with anyone else.'

'She won't have to.' Jane's mum beamed, happily. 'We've got it all worked out . . . she can have her own granny flat.'

After all her brave words to Lynn, Jane couldn't bring herself to break the news of what her mum and dad were planning. She still remembered the scorn with which Lynn had pronounced the words

14

'granny flat'. How she would crow! But with any luck, it would never happen. Mum and Dad were no more used to the country than Jane was; surely they would come to their senses once they had seen what it was like? No neighbours, no shops, no Chinese restaurants . . . just the horribly snooty green welly brigade, getting together every weekend to gallop across the countryside slaughtering everything that moved. Not that that aspect of it would bother her mum and dad, but even they must realize that the green wellies wouldn't want to know them? How could Mum have nice cosy chats over the garden fence? How could Dad go for his pint or play his round of golf? All the toffee-nosed wellies would jeer at them. The whole idea, thought Jane, was utterly ludicrous.

Unfortunately, what seemed ludicrous to Jane appeared to be highly desirable to her parents. She was appalled, on returning home from school the following day, to find her mum in a state of bubbling enthusiasm – 'Jane, I promise you . . . you won't be able to resist it!' – and her dad more excited than he'd been about anything since the day he had set up his new hi-fi system.

'Your mother's right. It's a gem.'

'Imagine, Janey! Waking up in the morning and seeing the Downs right outside your window!'

Jane shuddered, elaborately.

Her dad, vexed, said, 'She's set herself against it before we even go there!'

'Yes, because I don't want to go there! I like it here – I'm happy here!' Lynn was here, school was here, animal rights was here. She said as much, as heart-rendingly as she could, to her mum (her mum being by nature more sympathetic than her dad) but for once her mum refused to be moved.

'I've never cared over much for Lynn, if you want to know the truth, and the school's a crying disgrace. I'd have had you away from it years ago if we could have afforded it. As for that animal group – well! They all ought to be put behind bars, if you want my opinion. My heart's in my mouth every time you go anywhere with them.'

Jane clenched her fists, angrily. Just because most of them were out of work, and some of them had their heads shaved or wore gear that her mum considered peculiar, that didn't mean they were criminals, did it? They were people who were committed. They were people who *cared*. It was more than her mum did. She opened her mouth to say so, but her dad overrode her.

'All this is beside the point! I'm sorry if we're uprooting you, but you'll soon make new friends. You're not exactly a shrinking violet.'

'And there are some very good schools down there.'

A lump, partly of rage, partly of despair, rose into Jane's throat.

'You mean, you've actually decided?'

'We think so. We're pretty certain. We're going to go down there Christmas—'

'*Christmas?*'

'Just for a couple of weeks. To get the feel of the place before we finally make an offer.'

'Bed and breakfast?' shrieked Jane. 'At *Christmas*?'

'Not bed and breakfast.' That was her dad. 'Full board and lodging.'

16

'It's special for Christmas,' said Jane's mum. 'Live *en famille.'*

She pronounced it 'enn famill'. Jane, who had learnt good French at her supposed dump bin of a school, knew that it should be 'on famee'. She wished her mum wouldn't use foreign phrases if she didn't know how to say them properly. It would only give the green wellies something else to crow about.

'As family.' Jane said it irritably. 'I don't want to live as family!'

'They're awfully nice, Jane. Really! Lady Medd-Hall—'

'*Lady?*'

'Now, don't start!' begged her mum. 'We can do without one of your diatribes.'

'Yes, and we'll have none of it down at Shalla-ford! Lady Medd-Hall is an extremely pleasant woman – and capable, too. She's fought hard to keep that place going. It's not everyone in her position would have turned their hand to bed and break-fasting.'

Jane sniffed.

'Doesn't sound as though she's been very success-ful at it.'

'She's had a lot to cope with, Jane.' Her mum spoke reproachfully. 'She's had a lot of tragedy in her life. She lost her husband two years ago in a shooting accident.'

Jane regarded her mum, stonily. People who went shooting, in her opinion, deserved all they got. Her mum rushed hastily on.

'I don't know about you—' she turned to Jane's dad – 'but I had the feeling there was something else

17

. . . something about a son. I didn't like to ask, but I got the impression, from little things she let slip . . . as if perhaps he wasn't quite right.'

'Loopy, probably,' said Jane. 'Too much in-breeding. Makes them weak in the head.'

Her dad's finger shot out, angrily.

'Now, you just listen to me, young lady!'

'Woman, Dad, *please.*'

'Yes! Right. You're certainly no lady! Not a woman, either, if it comes to that. You're too im-mature. Like a spoilt child! I've had just about enough of your moaning. Your mum and I have worked hard all our lives. We've done our very best for you. You've never wanted for anything except a good school, and now when we're offering it to you all you can do is fling it in our faces!'

'But I'm happy where I am!' wailed Jane.

'You might be; your mum and I aren't. This is the first time we've ever asked anything for ourselves and we're not having you put the mockers on it! You can just get yourself in a better frame of mind and be a bit generous for once. There! I've had my say and I'll say no more. But I don't want to hear another whinge out of you, my girl!'

The only person she could moan at was Lynn, who, now that her prophecies had come true, could afford to be sympathetic.

'Gruesome,' she said, when Jane told her. 'Mind you, if you're going to be down there at Christmas you could always go and join the sabs at the Boxing Day meet.'

'What Boxing Day meet?'

'One in Lewes. It's advertised in the news-sheet.

18

They want as many anti-hunt supporters as they can get.'

Jane sighed. 'Yes; I could do that.'

'At least it would be something positive.'

'I suppose so.'

'Oh, look, cheer up!' said Lynn. 'It hasn't happened yet – they might decide against it.'

'They won't,' said Jane. 'I feel it in my bones.'

'What about your gran? What's she reckon to it? I shouldn't have thought she'd want to go and bury herself in the country.'

'No.' Jane brightened. Very much a townie, was Gran. She would be an ally for sure.

'It's a terrible thing,' urged Lynn, 'dragging some poor old girl away from everything she knows. Be like a living death.'

'For me as well,' said Jane.

'Worse for her. You'll get to university and get away from it all. She'll be stuck there till she dies.'

'It'll probably kill her,' said Jane. 'Either that or she'll lose her marbles.'

'It's criminal, really . . . way they treat old folk.'

'I'll go and see her,' said Jane.

Gran lived in a council flat just off the Goldhawk Road. It was on the sixth floor of a tower block and looked out on to another tower block. The lift smelt of unmentionable smells and the flat itself was dark and cramped, but Gran had lived there for fifteen years. She knew the people. She knew the area. Gran wouldn't want to leave her flat!

'Oh, wouldn't I?' said Gran, when Jane visited her that afternoon at the end of school. 'You want to try living here, my beauty! You wouldn't find it

19

such fun. Foreigners all over the place, every—'

'Gran!'

Jane cut in hastily before Gran could say something she ought not. It was an uncomfortable thing for a person of Jane's social outlook to admit, but the fact had to be faced: Gran was a terrible racist. (Of course, down in East Sussex there probably wouldn't be any skin to be seen save palest pink. Gran would like that.)

'What about the shops?' said Jane.

'Shops aren't what they were. All taken over by foreigners. Can't understand a word they say half the time.'

'But, Gran, think of the upheaval! You've lived in London all your life. You were born here, you got married here . . . surely you'd miss it?'

Gran considered.

'I might do – and there again, I might not. Some bits I'd miss . . . I'd miss the social. I'd miss me night out at the pub. I'd miss Mary McAllister popping in for a chat. Yes, I'd miss those things. I won't deny that.'

'Well, then!'

'But I'm getting on,' said Gran, 'and I wouldn't half mind a nice granny flat. After all, I'd still have me independence. And I'm all for new experiences, even at my age.'

'There won't *be* any new experiences,' moaned Jane. 'It'll be like living in a hole in the ground . . . we'll be dead from the neck up! Nothing happening from one week to the next.'

'You never know till you try,' said Gran. 'Any rate, that's the way I look at it.'

2

The Lawlors drove down to Shallaford on Christmas Eve. Gran, like a sensible woman, had decided against coming with them: she was spending Christmas in her own flat, with Mary McAllister to keep her company.

'I'll come when me granny flat's ready,' said Gran, 'but I don't fancy sitting around with a bunch of toffs all over Christmas.'

Jane didn't fancy it, either, but Jane didn't have any choice.

'You're mad,' she said to her mum. 'It'll be all the horsey set, going out every day to kill.'

'Whatever they do,' said her dad, 'just remember that they've paid for the privilege. It's no business of yours. You keep your mouth shut.'

'Please, Janey!' Her mum squeezed her arm. 'Let's have a nice time. Don't ruin it for us. And, Janey . . . you couldn't take something pretty to wear, could you? Just for once?'

'I haven't got anything pretty,' said Jane. 'I'm not a pretty sort of person.'

'No, but you can look quite attractive,' pleaded her mum, 'when you take the trouble.'

To keep her mum happy she packed her best pair

of trousers and a white shirt, as well as her usual assortment of tops and leggings; she also packed her Doc Martens and her jeans, ready for the Boxing Day meet. She hadn't yet told her parents about the Boxing Day meet and she wasn't quite sure how she was going to get there, but if necessary, she thought, she would walk the twelve miles to Lewes and back. She would never be able to look Lynn in the face if she didn't go and do her bit, and anyway it would be one in the eye for the horsey set.

She travelled down in her current favourite gear of purple leggings and long ribbed top, with a wondrous hand-knitted scarf about ten metres long which she had found in a charity shop. Her dad had looked at her and seemed about to say something, but after a quick dig in the ribs from Mum changed his mind. Mum really didn't like trouble; she hated it when Jane and her dad started rowing.

They reached Shallaford shortly after five.

'Look, Janey!' said her mum. 'Look at the Downs! Aren't they beautiful?'

Jane could not deny that they had a bit more going for them than the Goldhawk Road. Even in the dark they were impressive, rolling away into the distance beneath the winter sky.

'And the air! Oh, Janey! Just smell it!'

Jane stepped out of the car and took a breath.

'Help!' She staggered against the bonnet in a pretend faint. 'How am I going to get by without my daily fix of carbon monoxide?'

'The wonder of it is,' said her dad, 'that we've all survived as long as we have . . . it's not till you get out to the country that you realize how you've been poisoning yourself all these years.'

'It's so pure,' said her mum. 'I can breathe properly!'

This is all propaganda, thought Jane. She walked round to open the boot. I am not going to be brainwashed.

Shallaford Hall looked just as it had in the newspaper cutting, solid, four-square, and ugly. It also looked vaguely menacing, though Jane couldn't quite decide how. The sheer bulk of it, perhaps; the great slab sides across which the ivy, like some obscene growth, crawled and clung; the massed banks of windows like eyeless sockets, blindly staring into the night; the clustered groups of chimney-pots behind their parapet, marching in ranks across the skyline.

Jane shivered.

'Mum,' she said, 'I don't like it!'

Her mum slipped an arm about her shoulders.

'Wait till you see it in daylight!'

They made their way up the stone steps to the front door. Tendrils of ivy, like birds' claws, clutched at Jane's face. She thrust them aside, with a shudder.

'Jane! Look!' Her mum caught at her hand. 'Look at the moon!'

Jane turned. As she did so, a black shape suddenly launched itself from a nearby clump of trees. It came straight at her, brushing her face as it sailed past. Jane just about managed to stop herself from shrieking.

'What was that?'

'Lord!' Her dad gave one of his rasping chuckles. (He rasped because he smoked too much; not because of pollution in Shepherd's Bush.) 'She doesn't even recognize an owl when she sees one!'

'Of course I do,' said Jane crossly. 'I just wasn't expecting it.'

'Beautiful creatures, owls,' said her mum. 'You'll see plenty of them round here.'

'Symbols of evil,' muttered Jane.

'Rubbish!' Her dad gave her an impatient push. 'Don't start any of that nonsense. We've come here to enjoy ourselves. I don't need you carrying on like the voice of doom. Just be quiet and behave yourself.'

The door was opened by a squat, shapeless, ginger-haired woman with a big moon face. She was wearing a pink overall with buttons down the front and Jane thought at first she was a servant but she turned out to be Lady Medd-Hall.

'Mr and Mrs Lawlor!' she said. 'Lovely to see you again! Do come in. Is this Jane?'

'Yes,' said Mum. 'Jane, this is Lady Medd-Hall.'

Lady Lump, thought Jane. A terrible temptation came over her to drop a curtsey and whine, 'Pleased to meet you, ma'am, I'm sure.' She managed to suppress it.

'Hi,' she said, holding out a hand.

Lady Medd-Hall took it and gave it a hearty wring. (Weren't the gentry supposed just barely to *touch*? Jane was sure she had read somewhere that hearty handshakes were confined to the unwashed masses.)

'Glad to see you, Jane. I hope you're going to like it here.' I bet you do, thought Jane. After all, you want to sell the place. 'Come in, and I'll get Andrew to show you to your rooms. I've given you and Mr Lawlor the one we discussed when you were down here, Mrs Lawlor, dear – the one you liked so much

– and I've given Jane the one next to it. I thought you'd like to be near each other – Ah, Andrew, there you are!'

A youth had appeared through one of the doors opening off the entrance hall. He looked to be about Jane's age, maybe a year or two older. Jane's heart, in spite of herself, turned over at the sight of him. He had to be called beautiful; there was no other word for it. Tall, rather slight. But perfectly proportioned: dark hair, falling romantically in a lock over one eye; narrow face with classical features; small straight nose, generous mouth curving upwards in an attractively crooked smile.

Jane swallowed, and touched instinctively, without even realizing that she was doing it, at her hair. (Jane's hair was blonde, or at any rate blondeish. It was long and rather straggly, except when freshly washed. She wished now that she had taken the trouble to wash it before leaving home, but she had been in too much of a sulk at the time.)

Andrew strolled, smiling, across the parquet floor.

'This is my nephew,' said Lady Lump. 'Andrew, Mr and Mrs Lawlor—'

'I remember you.' Andrew held out a hand: slender and well-manicured.

'And this is their daughter,' said Lady Lump. 'Jane.'

'How do you do?' Andrew turned the full power of his lopsided smile upon her. Jane felt her cheeks fire up. She was uncomfortably conscious of the fact, as she had not been with Lady Lump, that her own hands were far from being well-manicured. She still had a childish habit of chewing her fingernails.

'Andrew, would you show Mr and Mrs Lawlor to the Elizabeth room?'

'Sure.' Andrew stooped, to pick up the suitcases.

'I've put Jane next door. I hope you'll find everything you want there, Jane. Don't hesitate to tell me if there's anything you need. We're still a bit basic here, I'm afraid. We've never quite moved with the times.'

'Ah, but that's the charm of the place,' said Jane's mum.

Jane cringed. She did hope her mum wasn't going to *creep*.

They followed beautiful Andrew up the stairs – threadbare carpet, noted Jane. To their right, on the first landing, a long passage ran the length of the house, with doors opening off it on either side. Immediately opposite, at the head of the stairs, was a large picture window looking out on to the grounds at the back; while to the left, on the same side as the window, were two more doors and a smaller one, right at the end, which most probably, Jane thought, opened on to a cupboard.

'Elizabeth room.' Andrew stopped at the second door along. '*Et pour vous, Mademoiselle—*' with a flourish and a mock bow, he threw open a door for Jane – 'the Boudoir!'

'Pardon?' said Jane.

'Boudoir.' He pronounced it with an exageratedly French accent. 'Where Mademoiselle may sit, if she wish, and *boude*. If she is given to *bouding, bien sûr*. Are you given to *bouding?*'

Jane hesitated, wanting to make some smart comeback but for the life of her unable to remember what the word meant.

26

'*Mais non!*' Andrew waved his hands, in French-ified fashion. 'Mademoiselle does not look like a leetle sulky one . . . she is all sunshine and light; no?'

'No!' roared Jane's dad, from the room next door. 'All rain and hailstorms, more like.'

Really, there were times when Jane could cheerfully have throttled her dad.

'Actually,' said Andrew, reverting to his normal speaking voice (what Lynn would call posh), 'I refer to it as the Boudoir because it used to be a lady's dressing room. I have to apologize for the size of it. You can have a bigger one, if you want. We've loads going begging. Aunt clings to this belief that all young gels like to be safely under the wing of their parents. She thought you might be a bit fazed being on your own at the other end of the corridor.'

'I wouldn't,' said Jane, 'but this'll do me fine.' It was at least three times as big as her room at home.

'Well, if you're sure,' said Andrew. 'I'll leave you to get settled in. Bathroom's the last door on the right, by the way. See you at dinner!'

Did one have to dress for dinner? Jane wondered, nervously. Her mum hadn't said anything about it, and indeed, if she had, Jane would only have jumped down her throat.

'Dress for *dinner*? You must be joking!'

But if everyone else did and she didn't, she was going to look pretty silly. Lynn would say that by not doing so she would be making a political statement, and that was what Jane herself would have said up until about five minutes ago. Now she wasn't quite so sure that she wanted to make political statements.

She dumped her case on the bed and looked at

herself in the winged mirror standing on the chest of drawers. God, but her hair was a mess! Where had he said the bathroom was? At the end of the corridor?

Jane seized her sponge bag and shampoo and scuttled off down there. The corridor was longer than the whole of the Lawlors' house plus front and back gardens put together. The bathroom looked as if it might once have been a bedroom. It was large, but primitive; far more primitive than the bathroom at home. On the other hand, it did have carpet on the floor and a battered wicker chair to sit in.

Jane washed her hair hurriedly, remembered too late that she should have brought her towel with her (her mum had warned her before they came, 'It's not going to be like a hotel, you know'), wrung herself out as best she could and raced back, dripping, to her room.

She couldn't dress for dinner because she didn't have a dress, but she put on her best black trousers and her starched white shirt with the high pointy collar and did her hair in a plait, which made her look sophisticated, and although she still couldn't be described as pretty (she wouldn't want to be described as pretty; pretty was vapid) she thought the effect wasn't too bad.

Jane was not someone who bothered much as a rule about her appearance. She dressed for comfort and to show where her allegiances lay: with animal rights and the left. She wasn't silly about boys, either. She'd had a sort of boyfriend, Sean, in the West London Animal Action Group, but he'd gone off back to Ireland and since then there hadn't been anyone special. She wasn't the sort of girl to wilt if she didn't have someone to sigh over. She didn't believe in allowing her life to revolve around men; in fact she rather prided herself that she could take them or leave them. On the other hand, that didn't mean to say that she was totally immune.

At seven o'clock, her mum knocked on her door.

'Oh, Janey!' she said. 'You do look nice!'

Jane scowled. She wished her mum wouldn't. She knew she meant well, but still she wished she wouldn't.

'We're going down to have a drink. Are you coming?'

They went back down the threadbare-carpeted stairs to the main entrance hall. Jane saw that two of the doors leading off it bore notices saying 'Private'. She wondered what lay behind them. Luxuries untold – or more of the threadbare carpet?

Her mum tugged at her sleeve. 'Jane, that area's private!'

'We'll partition it off properly,' said Dad, 'if we buy the place.'

Andrew, coming down the stairs, could hardly have avoided hearing the remark. Jane felt like dying of embarrassment. Her dad, of course, having a hide like a rhinoceros, showed no signs of discomfiture.

'I was just saying,' said Dad, 'you could do with a bit more demarcation between your quarters and the rest of the house. You must find it a right pain, having punters wandering about all over the place.'

Andrew very slightly hunched a shoulder. (But had Jane seen his lip curl?)

'My aunt's a very sociably-minded woman. She likes to meet people.'

'All the same,' said Dad.

29

'Let me get you a drink.' Andrew moved smoothly ahead of them across the hall. 'Mrs Lawlor, gin and tonic, as I recall?'

The bar was built into one corner of a room furnished with a selection of sagging easy chairs and a battered sofa covered in dog and cat hairs. There was a television in another corner, which to Jane's mortification her dad immediately switched on. She wished that just for once he wouldn't: watching television was definitely naff. Jane herself asked for a fresh orange juice and went to sit in solitary splendour on the window seat, with a copy of yesterday's *Times* which someone had left there. *The Times* didn't quite give the right political image, but at least it showed that she had mastered words of more than two syllables.

Almost at once they were joined by other guests – a party of four adults, two of whom were middle-aged and married, two of whom were younger but not, as far as Jane could make out from her vantage point behind *The Times*, particularly struck on each other. The married ones, who were called Bland, turned out to run a riding stable. The younger ones, a pimply youth called Graham and a pasty plump girl called Patsy, were people who rode at the riding stable. They had all, to Jane's disgust, come to Shallaford for the hunting. She heard them talking about it to Andrew.

'Will you be joining us?' said Patsy, leaning all plump and pasty over the bar.

Jane strained her ears to hear Andrew's reply, but all she caught was Patsy's, 'Oh, what a shame!'

Jane put down her *Times* and went over to her parents.

'Dad,' said Jane, 'you couldn't drive me into Lewes on Boxing Day, could you, and come and pick me up again afterwards?'

'On Boxing Day? What on earth for?'

'There's an anti-hunt demo.' Jane didn't bother to keep her voice down. 'I want to go to it.'

Her dad's face grew mottled.

'No, I will not drive you into Lewes!' He leaned over towards her. 'You just watch it, my girl! I won't tolerate any of that sort of nonsense while we're under someone else's roof.'

Why not? thought Jane. They were paying to be there, weren't they? She went back to *The Times*, and to her orange juice. She hadn't actually expected Dad to drive her into Lewes, and if her dad wouldn't, her mum almost certainly wouldn't, either. She would ask Andrew for a map, she thought. Twelve miles shouldn't be beyond her.

At eight o'clock Lady Medd-Hall appeared and brightly announced that dinner was ready.

'With something special for Jane, because she's a vegan.' Everyone turned to stare, as if she had declared that Jane was an alien from outer space. 'Oh, we cater for all tastes here!' said Lady Medd-Hall. 'We had a lady once on a gluten-free diet. Didn't turn a hair! Did we?'

Andrew shook his head, in confirmation. 'We're still awaiting our first cannibal.'

'Silly boy!' His aunt aimed a flick at him with the cloth she was holding. She had removed her pink overall but really could not be said to have dressed for the occasion. Her tweed skirt was all baggy where she sat down, and her cardigan had lost all its shape (rather like Lady Medd-Hall

31

herself). In fact nobody, Jane was relieved to note, was exactly dressed for the occasion. Andrew was the smartest person present. He was actually wearing a collar and tie and a jacket. Lynn would have sniffed and said 'Poncy!' but it made a change, thought Jane, from shaven heads and T-shirts.

A girl was in the dining room, laying out knives and forks. (There were also two shaggy dogs hopefully circling the table, and five cats sitting in a row on top of the sideboard. Jane clicked her fingers at them. She sometimes thought she preferred animals to people.)

Lady Medd-Hall, in what seemed to Jane a somewhat casual manner – quite different from her oozing benevolence towards Andrew – introduced the girl as 'My daughter, Helen. The same age as you, Jane. Why don't you sit together? Then you can chat.'

Jane had the feeling that Helen wanted to chat to her no more than she wanted to chat to Helen. She was a thin, intense-looking girl, dark-haired and black-browed, more like her cousin Andrew than her moon-faced mother; but whereas Andrew's features were regular, Helen's were an odd assortment of shapes and sizes. Her eyes, which were so dark as to be almost black, were small and deep set; her nose was prominent; her mouth wide with a full, pouting bottom lip. She and Jane, in unspoken agreement, seated themselves at opposite ends of the table. To Jane's irritation, big pasty Patsy wangled herself next to Andrew. (She was *years* too old for him, and anyway he wouldn't look twice at a huge lumbering thing like that.) Jane found herself wedged in between horsey Mr Bland and her mum.

While they were eating, sounds of music drifted into the room.

'Now, what is that?' said Mrs Bland. 'Don't tell me! Let me guess . . . it's not the Beatles, that's for sure!'

'Mozart.' Helen muttered it, so low as to be almost inaudible. Mrs Bland leaned towards her, cupping a hand to her ear.

'Mozart? Lovely!' She sat back, making rapt piano-playing motions on the table with her fingers. 'So much nicer than all that head-banging stuff.'

Jane, who wasn't musical and couldn't have told Mozart from Mahler, hardly noticed it, what with Mr Bland going on about fetlocks on one side of her and her mum wittering about food on the other.

'How is your nut loaf, Jane? Is it good? It looks good. I must get the recipe; mine always seem to fall to pieces. Are those walnuts, or are they cashews? They look like cashews. I must try cashews next time. Cashews and hazelnuts; they should go well together.'

Jane sat in silence, feeding bits of her nut loaf to the two shaggy dogs underneath the table and listening to the hubbub of voices. Everyone was talking except her and the girl Helen. Even her dad was making an effort. Helen sat hunched over her food, scarcely raising her eyes from her plate. She looked, decided Jane, thoroughly disagreeable. Unlike her mother, she obviously didn't care for people. Well, that suited Jane; she didn't care so terribly much for people, either, so that made two of them.

A temporary lull in the hubbub allowed the music to be heard.

'Wonderful darling Mozart!' cried Mrs Bland.

Don't like Mozart, thought Jane. *Tinkles*. And anyway, it was élitist.

'By gum!' That was her dad's voice, suddenly booming out across the table. 'This sounds pretty tasty! What are you using?' He looked at Andrew. 'Valves? Or solid state?'

There was a silence. Jane inwardly writhed. Don't say Dad was going to start on about hi-fi and bore everyone to death.

'Um—' Andrew flicked his eyes, uncertainly, towards Helen.

'Valves,' said Helen. She said it shortly, not bothering to look up.

Jane's dad, who never recognized a snub and was therefore virtually unsnubbable, leaned forward eagerly.

'I thought it had to be! You'd never get solid state to sound like that. What have you got?'

Slowly, Helen raised her eyes from her plate.

'Something I built myself. From circuit diagrams.'

'Built it yourself? Well, I never!' said Dad.

Jane could tell, from the way he said it, that he was secretly marvelling at the fact that a mere female should be capable of such a feat. A dull blush spread over Helen's rather sullen features.

'It's based on an old Mullard design.'

'Mullard! Blow me!' Dad gave one of his throaty chuckles. 'That takes me back a bit! What sort of current does it shift?'

'Forty amps.'

'As much as that? That's a lot of power!'

34

'The same as ring mains,' said Helen.

Andrew, catching Jane's eye across the table, tapped a finger to his forehead. The hubbub had started up again, but at intervals, cutting across the horse talk and the food talk, Jane caught odd snippets of hi-fi babble – sub-woofer, output transformers, PCBs, electrostatics. Helen was sitting up straight, giving as good as she got. She was really turned on by it, thought Jane.

'That is one smart young lady,' said Jane's dad, as they retired after dinner to the guests' sitting room. 'Not often you find a girl who's into electronics.'

Christmas Day was strange; the first one Jane had ever spent away from home. She felt that they had already celebrated proper Christmas with Gran, before coming down to Shallaford. They had all gone round to Gran's place and had their Christmas dinner, the same as usual (with Jane just eating vegetables, because Gran didn't hold with pandering to fads and fancies and concocting special dishes: to her, vegetarianism was cranky). Dad had bought a bottle of pink champagne and a big fat cigar and Mum had had her egg flip and Gran had had her port and lemon and afterwards they had sat round the telly in a fug, with Jane inwardly railing, as she always did, at the boredom of it all. Every Christmas she swore that, 'Next Christmas I'm going to do something different.' And now here she was, doing something different, and not at all sure how she felt about it.

It didn't seem right, for a start, to open presents in your bedroom; yet it would have seemed even less right to open them downstairs in full view of strangers.

Lynn had given her a joke present – a small glass jar full of mud. On it she had stuck a label saying 'Shepherd's Bush Earth: to remind you of your origins'. And in a card accompanying it she had written, 'What does one buy for the girl who has everything?' Jane hoped it was just Lynn being funny; she couldn't bear to think that Mum and Dad coming into money would change their relationship. She was glad now that she had only bought Lynn a Cruelty Free diary and nothing too showy. It would have seemed vulgar to have splashed out, and anyway it might have made Lynn feel resentful.

Gran, totally unmoved by the family's new-found riches, had given her a hand-knitted sweater. Gran's knitting was rather loose and sloppy, with the odd dropped stitch because she couldn't see too well, and when she had been younger Jane had always complained bitterly at being expected to put things on on Christmas Day 'So that Gran can see you in them'. Today she felt such a rush of affection as she unpacked the shapeless object that she was very nearly tempted to wear it down to breakfast; but then she thought that Gran wasn't here to see it and everyone else would be bound to be done up like a dog's dinner, and really and truly Gran's knitting wasn't the sort of thing that ought to be displayed in public. It was for private wear, when you wanted to curl up with a book and be sloblike.

Mum and Dad had given her a cheque for five hundred pounds. Jane had never had so much money in her life. Her first thought was that she would go out and blow the lot on clothes: her second that she would donate part of it to NAVS*. The idea made her happy: Lynn would approve of it.

First thing after breakfast they telephoned Gran in Shepherd's Bush – 'Enjoying yourselves?' said Gran. 'With all the nobs?' – and then went out for a walk on the Downs. Jane would have liked to have taken the dogs with them but the dogs, it seemed, were going with Helen – who manifestly had no desire to join forces. Well, that was all right, thought Jane: she had no desire to join forces with Helen. But she would have liked to have taken the dogs.

Christmas lunch was a bit grander than at Gran's, with special nut cutlets provided for Jane's benefit and high-class crackers with proper presents such as key rings and miniature mouth organs. Mum went all upmarket and asked for dry sherry instead of egg flip, though Jane could see from the prunelike shape of her mouth that she didn't really enjoy it; and Dad, magnanimous at the end of the meal, handed round some of his big cigars.

Over coffee the horrible hunting people discussed their plans for Boxing Day. Jane, with an effort, bit her tongue; not so much out of deference to being under someone else's roof as for her mum's sake. She knew Mum would sink with shame if she said anything. She had made up her mind that before the day was out she would definitely ask Andrew for a map, but as they were leaving the room he came up to her.

'Did I hear you say last night that you wanted to go into Lewes tomorrow?'

*National Anti-Vivisection Society

37

'Yes.' Jane looked at him, defiantly. He might be beautiful, but she didn't intend to compromise her principles. 'For the anti-hunt demo.'

'Sh!' He raised a finger to his lips. 'Not in this house! This is Bloodsports Hall. But I'll drive you in, if you want. I have to go in anyway, with the horsebox.'

Jane tilted her chin.

'I can always walk,' she said.

'Why do that when I'm offering you a lift?'

'Well, but if you don't support the cause—'

'Who said I didn't?'

'You mean, you do?'

He closed one eye in a wink.

'Be ready for ten o'clock. I'll see you get there.'

Well! That was a turn-up for the books, thought Jane. Her dad could hardly complain when it was Lady Medd-Hall's own nephew who was taking her.

Mum and Dad spent the rest of the afternoon watching television, while Jane yawned and read a book and looked at the television and pulled faces and went back to her book and wondered if being at Shallaford was more or less boring than being at Gran's. Next year, she thought, I shall do something different.

In the evening Lady Medd-Hall and Andrew – but not Helen – reappeared from behind locked doors with mince pies and much evidence of good will.

'Games!' announced Lady Medd-Hall, brightly. 'We always play games at Christmas!'

'Oh, lovely!' cried Mum, who in fact liked nothing better than to fug in front of the television.

Andrew caught Jane's eye and very slightly

turned down the corners of his mouth. Jane, the ultimate in coolness and sophistication, gave a little grimace. Games, for heaven's sake! How Lynn would laugh.

Under Lady Medd-Hall's supervision they played relentlessly until midnight – not poker or gin rummy, which was what they sometimes played at Gran's – but charades and *Scrabble* and *Trivial Pursuit*, and something which Lady Medd-Hall called *Dumb Crambo*, which simply meant acting things out without words.

'So much more fun than just sitting goggling at the box all night,' said Jane's mum, as they went upstairs. 'You must admit, Janey!'

Jane was the one who had never *wanted* to goggle at the box.

'It really hasn't been as awful as you thought, has it? Come on! Be fair!' Mum whispered roguishly in Jane's ear: 'With a young man like that about the place?'

'Oh, Mum!' said Jane. 'For heaven's sake!'

The evening had been OK. It had been passable. Lady Medd-Hall had jollied them all along, and pasty Patsy had got tight, and Mrs Bland had inadvertently made a rude word at *Scrabble*, which everyone had ribbed her about. Even charades hadn't been too bad. Jane and Andrew had done one together in which Andrew had played Richard III as a hunch-backed cripple with a club foot and Jane had been the Princes in the Tower being smothered by him. It had all gone rather mad and over the top but at least it had made people laugh, though really it had been Andrew who had done most of the acting: Jane had just been a stooge. She had enjoyed it all right, far more than she had anticipated; but that still didn't mean she wanted to leave London and come and bury herself at Shallaford.

'Give it a chance,' said her mum. 'It'll grow on you. You'll see!'

Surprisingly, for as a rule she lay awake reading for at least an hour before going to sleep, Jane's eyes closed almost the minute she climbed into bed. (How could fresh air be good for you if all it did was tire you out?)

The sleep that she slept was full of dreams; full of owls slowly flapping across the night sky and tendrils of ivy which grew into ropes and wound themselves about her legs as she walked. She couldn't make out where it was that she was walking, except that it was somewhere high up, and narrow, like a mountain pass, only she didn't think it was a mountain pass. The vast black shape which rose behind her had not the look of a mountain. As she strove in her dream to identify it – a slag heap? Was that how a slag heap might look? – a voice called out to her in warning.

'I can see you, Jane! Be careful!'

Jane stirred in her sleep. For just a moment her eyelids fluttered open and she lay still, in the darkness, listening; but nothing was there and almost immediately she slipped away again, back to the narrow pass with the black shape behind it and the ropes of ivy which trailed and clung – and the same voice as before, whispering in her ear.

'I wouldn't go to sleep if I were you, Jane . . . I'm watching you, Jane! I wouldn't go to sleep!'

The ivy, now, was in thick coils, writhing and

twisting like snakes. Jane kicked out in a frenzy, thrashing her legs as she tried to free herself. Next thing she knew, in her panic, in the manner of dreams, she was plunging, headfirst, into the void.

A shrill shriek of laughter echoed through her head.

'I'm going to get you, Jane . . . I'm going to get you!'

Jane shot up the bed, heart hammering. She snapped on the bedside lamp.

'I'm going to get you, Jane!'

Was it really a voice? Or was she just imagining it?

She sat, tense and hunched, eyes straining to see into the shadows which lay beyond the small circle of light cast by the lamp.

Not a murmur. Not a movement.

Jane pulled a face. What had she expected? The door was locked; who could get in?

Nobody could get in. She was behaving like a tit.

She reached out a hand to turn off the lamp. It was then that she heard it . . . the sound of tapping.

Tap: tap tap. Tap: tap tap.

It was coming from outside the window, almost as if someone – some *thing* – were out there, trying to attract attention; only of course that was absurd. No-one could be outside a window on the first floor. It just wasn't possible.

The tapping went on. *Tap: tap tap. Tap: tap tap.* It was an eerie sound in the silence of the sleeping house. *Tap: tap tap. Tap: tap tap.*

A tree! It had to be a tree. A tree outside the window.

Was there a tree outside the window?

Jane was not a girl to be easily intimidated. Boldly, she flung back the bedclothes (no duvets at Shallaford Hall), padded across to the window and threw open the curtains.

'*Oh!*'

What she saw caused her to spring back, a hand pressed to her mouth to stifle the scream that rose within her. Bobbing up and down, at the level of the windowsill, were two faces. She could just make out the eyes, and white teeth gleaming in the darkness.

Jane turned, and ran.

3

'Faces at the window?' Dad, in his pyjamas, with Mum a few paces behind, hurriedly pulling on her dressing-gown, trod stolidly down the corridor to Jane's room. 'What are you talking about, girl? You're six metres off the ground!'

'Dad, there were,' said Jane. 'I'm not making it up! I saw them, peering over the windowsill.'

'Rubbish!' Dad marched across the room, threw up both windows and leaned out, into the night. 'Hello! Is there anybody there?'

'Neil, quiet! You'll wake people up.'

'Well, really . . . faces at the window! You just take a look.' Dad stepped back to make way for Jane, nervously hovering at his elbow. 'Just take a look and tell me how anyone could possibly peer over that windowsill. They couldn't! Not unless they were six metres tall or standing on a ladder. And if you can see any signs of a ladder—'

'There could have been! They could have taken it away again.'

'To what end?'

'Well – I don't know! They could have been burglars, or something.'

'Burglars don't go round hefting filthy great

43

ladders in the middle of the night. Not when they know a house is occupied.'

'Are you sure you weren't just having a nightmare, lovey?'

'I don't have nightmares,' muttered Jane. It was true she had been dreaming – something about owls and ropes of ivy – but it was real tapping that had woken her up.

'It does sometimes happen,' said her mum. 'Sleeping in a strange bed—'

'Mum, there were faces! I saw them! They were horrible.'

'Begins to sound like a visit from Chelsea football supporters!' Her dad gave one of his throaty rasps. 'How many were there? A whole horde?'

'Two.' Jane said it resentfully. It was plain that neither Mum nor Dad believed her. She could have understood it if she'd been the sort to indulge in fantasies, but she wasn't; she didn't have that sort of imagination. In fact she didn't have much imagination at all. Whenever she watched horror movies with Lynn, it was always Lynn who sat with her eyes screwed tight shut at all the nastiest moments. Boring old Jane could never quite forget that it was only a movie.

'I'll tell you what,' said Dad. 'What's the betting it was just a couple of owls being nosy?'

Owls! Did her dad think she was such an unredeemed townie that she couldn't even recognize an owl when she saw one? All right, so she hadn't that first day but that was because it had come at her unexpectedly, out of the darkness.

'Be honest.' Dad pulled the windows shut and

bolted them. 'An owl peering through . . . you'd think it was a face.'

'Not with teeth,' muttered Jane.

'Well, whatever it was, it's not there now – and even if it were it couldn't get at you.'

'Are you sure you'll be all right?' Her mum took Jane's hand, coaxing her back to bed. 'You don't want your dad to come in here, and you come in with me?'

Jane shook her head. Already she was starting to feel ashamed of herself. It wasn't like her to panic and go running to her mum and dad. Even when she was little and had been frightened by giant spiders galloping across the ceiling she had simply crept further down the bed and prayed they wouldn't drop on her.

'If you keep the curtains drawn—'

'They were drawn! I heard this tapping, that's what woke me.'

'Owls,' said her dad. 'Beaks tapping on glass.'

Owls, thought Jane, pulling the bedclothes over her head, did not have *teeth*.

In spite of possessing no imagination, Jane found it difficult to relax and go back to sleep. She lay curled up beneath the bedclothes, straining her ears for every sound. She heard footsteps along the corridor – slow and stealthy over the creaking floorboards. At any other time she would have known that it was only someone visiting the bathroom, treading quietly so as not to disturb people. Tonight it could have been anything from a headless ghost to a madman on the prowl.

She heard doors open and close. She heard voices,

disembodied, murmuring and squeaking: she heard *things* outside, dragging and grating. Common sense would ordinarily have told her that in a house full of people doors might well open and close, even in the middle of the night; that the disembodied voices obviously came from a radio, and that the things outside were perfectly normal country sorts of things, such as badgers, or foxes, going about their normal night-time business.

Unfortunately, for once, Jane's common sense let her down. She kept remembering her dream; the shrill shriek of laughter and the voice that whispered in her ear.

'I'm going to get you, Jane . . . I'm going to get you!'

It was almost morning before she fell asleep.

She was woken by her mum, gaily rattling back the curtains.

'Lazybones! Time to get up!'

Jane groaned – and then remembered that it was Boxing Day and she had business to attend to.

'No more Chelsea supporters?' said her mum, teasing.

Jane smiled, and shook her head, willing to go along with the joke for what was the point of protesting? Already the events of the night had taken on an air of unreality. It was a temptation to wipe them from her memory, to pretend they had never happened – except that she knew very well that they had. She *knew* she had heard a voice: she *knew* she had seen faces at the window. And yet how could she have done, without believing in the supernatural?

'Breakfast in ten minutes!' sang her mum.

'Yes, all right,' said Jane. 'I'm coming.'

Quickly she pulled on her demo gear – thick sweater and jeans and her non-leather Doc Martens – splashed some water over her face, grabbed her anorak and headed downstairs. The supernatural would have to wait.

Everyone was at breakfast save Helen. The hunting fraternity were there, all done up in their black jackets and their jodhpurs, gobbling down their rashers of dead pig as fast as they could go. Lady Medd-Hall was there, wearing her pink nylon smock with the buttons down the front. Mum and Dad were there, looking anxious lest Jane should open her mouth and disgrace them. Andrew was there, elegant as ever in sweater and slacks. He grinned at Jane across the table and closed one eye in a conspiratorial wink. Jane grinned back. She hadn't yet told Mum and Dad what she was planning to do.

'Help yourself, dear.' Lady Medd-Hall shunted the toast rack towards Jane. 'Don't be backward, we don't stand on any ceremony here. I trust we all had a good night's sleep?'

Heads nodded round the table. Bulging mouths signified agreement.

'How about Jane? Did she have a good night's sleep?'

'Well . . . not really,' said Jane.

'Oh, my dear! Why was that?'

Jane felt Mum's foot pressing a warning against hers. But it was all right, she wasn't going to mention the faces. She didn't want to be laughed at, thank you very much.

'Someone was playing a radio. It kept me awake for hours.'

'Well, that was very naughty of someone,' said Lady Medd-Hall. 'Who was it? Own up!'

Andrew tugged at his forelock.

'Not guilty, ma'am!'

'It certainly wasn't me,' said Patsy. She giggled. 'You know the state I was in when I went to bed!'

'I went straight to sleep,' said Graham.

'Me, too,' said Mrs Bland. 'I must admit, I slept soundly all night. Didn't hear a thing.'

'You must have been imagining it,' said Mum.

She hadn't; she hadn't imagined the radio any more than she had imagined the faces. But at least there was a rational explanation for the radio (*one* of them must have been playing it). There wasn't any explanation for the faces.

'Does this house have ghosts?' she said.

'Oh, I daresay it might have the odd galumping Cavalier – it was built on the site of an Elizabethan manor, you know.' Lady Medd-Hall volunteered the information more to Dad than to Jane, obviously thinking it might increase his interest in the property. She was right: it did. Dad leapt in immediately. He was a sucker for anything like that.

'Jane,' whispered her mum, 'don't start talking about ghosts . . . I'm sure it was only an owl.'

After breakfast, because she had time to spare before setting off for Lewes, Jane went into the garden to examine the ground directly beneath her bedroom window. If there was no supernatural explanation – and really and truly she didn't believe in ghosts – then there had to be a natural one, and a ladder was the only thing she could think of.

Bushes grew all along the back wall of the house. Jane didn't know their names, but most of them were green in spite of it being winter, and some of them were prickly. The ones that grew beneath her window were especially prickly, so that no-one could have climbed them even if they had grown tall enough, which in any case they didn't.

Cautiously, keeping away from the prickles, Jane crouched on hands and knees on the gravel path, trying to peer behind the bushes and check for ladder marks in the earth. It was difficult to be sure, but as far as she could make out there didn't seem to be any, which there almost certainly would have been if a ladder had borne the weight of two people.

She was just scrambling to her feet when a cheerful voice said, 'I should watch it, if I were you! That's berberis.'

Jane turned, scarlet-faced and feeling foolish, to find Andrew standing there.

'Nasty stuff, berberis.' He regarded her quizzically, one eyebrow cocked. 'Have you lost something, by any chance? Or are you digging for buried treasure?'

She scrambled hastily to her feet.

'I thought I saw something.' She wasn't going to tell even Andrew about the faces at the window. He seemed sympathetic but like everyone else he would probably only jump to the conclusion that she had been hallucinating. She wouldn't want him running away with the idea that she was some kind of hysterical female.

'What sort of something? Nice or nasty?'

Jane laughed. 'Just a cat, I expect. Is it time to set off?'

'We'll be loading the horses in about five minutes.'

'I'll go and tell Mum and Dad.'

Jane ran back into the house. Mum was playing a game of Patience, Dad already seated in front of the telly.

'I'm going into Lewes with Andrew.' She whispered it at her mum. 'Is that OK?'

Mum nodded, smiling. 'Have a nice time!'

Just for a moment Jane felt a pang of conscience. She wasn't duty bound to tell her mum what she was planning, but all the same it was a sort of deceit. Poor old Mum thinking it was normal boy-meets-girl-asks-girl-out (probably already cherishing secret daydreams if the truth were known); not the least idea that her renegade daughter was hotfooting it to Lewes to join the horrible hunt sabs and jeer at the lovely hunters – including four of Lady Medd-Hall's own guests. Dad would go berserk if he found out, which no doubt he would when the horsey bunch came back. Oh, well! It couldn't be helped. Principles were principles; they didn't always make for an easy life.

Andrew was waiting for her at the wheel of the horsebox. (The Blands, with Patsy and Graham, were to follow in the Blands' Rover.)

'You'll have to forgive me,' said Andrew, as they set off, slowly because of the horses, down the gravel drive, 'if I dump you and leave you. I'll come back and pick you up again, of course. But I daren't join in the actual demo, much as I'd like to. Wouldn't be good publicity for Aunt Elinor. All the locals round here are well into hunting. Bloodthirsty bunch. Not at all the sort of place for a nice girl like you to come and live.'

'You don't hunt?' said Jane.

'Me? Would I be taking you on this gig if I did?'

No; she supposed not.

'Whatever you do, by the way, don't bring the subject up in front of Helen or my aunt. I told you, Shallaford is Bloodsports Hall – and besides, they do have a living to make.'

Jane's lip curled. Having a living to make was no excuse for tearing living creatures to pieces.

'If someone sees me,' she said, 'they're bound to mention it, but don't worry . . . I won't bring you into it. You can pretend I told you that I just wanted to go into Lewes to look at everyone on their horses.'

'Too kind!' murmured Andrew.

'Well, but I can see it might be difficult for you.'

'I'm sure you must think I'm the most terrible coward. It's just that I happen to be extremely fond of Aunt Elinor; I'd hate to do anything which might upset her. She's already had quite enough tragedy in her life.'

Jane thought, it could hardly be counted *tragedy* that her nephew didn't share her own bloodthirsty views on what constituted sport.

'What about Helen?' she said.

'Oh! Helen. Well—' Andrew raised both hands from the steering-wheel. 'Changing the subject slightly, what made you ask about ghosts this morning?'

'I—' Jane hesitated. 'I kept hearing these strange noises in the night.'

'If you're referring to the radio, it was probably Helen tinkering with her electronics.'

Yes, thought Jane, it would be Helen. She wouldn't care if she disturbed the guests. She obviously held them all in total contempt, sitting there at dinner with a face as long as a kite, not deigning to talk to anyone. Snooty piece.

'I'm afraid Helen's a bit of an oddball,' said Andrew. 'She doesn't sleep too well so she tends to wander and tinker and just generally make mayhem. I'm sorry if she kept you awake. I'll have a word with her.'

'Oh, there's no need,' said Jane. 'I wouldn't normally have noticed it, it's just that . . . something woke me up and then I couldn't get back to sleep again.'

'And you thought there might be ghosts?'

'Not seriously.'

'There usually are,' said Andrew, 'in old houses. I've never actually heard of any at Shallaford, but it wouldn't surprise me if—' He stopped.

'If what?'

'Well! Houses are living entities, aren't they?'

'Are they?' said Jane.

'Oh, I think so! They're not just bricks and mortar; there's more to them than that. It wouldn't surprise me if the poor old place were gathering its forces.'

Jane looked at him. 'What for?'

'To defend itself! It's been around for a century and a half. I don't imagine it's exactly rejoicing in the prospect of being tampered with.'

'What, you mean if Mum and Dad buy it?'

'They'd have to make certain changes, wouldn't they? If they were going to turn it into a proper hotel.'

'Guest house,' said Jane.

'Guest house, hotel . . . whichever. As your dad said, they'd want to block off the private quarters, for a start. Then I guess they'd have to split the rooms up – it's hardly a paying proposition the way it is now.'

'Maybe they won't buy it,' said Jane.

'You reckon?'

She sighed. 'Not really. Mum's dead set on it.'

'And you?'

'Not me!' Jane shook her head, vigorously. 'I'm quite happy where I am.'

'I guess you must find the country pretty dead after London.'

'It's OK for visiting.' She was anxious not to be thought ungracious. 'It's just that I wouldn't actually want to live here.'

'No; I can understand that.'

His tone indicated that he might be in sympathy. 'How about you?' she said. 'Have you always lived here?'

'Me? No; not always.'

'So—' She bit the question back, feeling suddenly that perhaps it might be considered intrusive. He answered it anyway.

'Why am I here now? Because, my dear—' he spoke in a mock drawl – 'I am the only Man left in the family. The only man still capable, that is. Being a man does have its drawbacks . . . you'd be surprised.'

'Yes, I would,' said Jane.

'I thought you would. Seriously, though, my aunt's been through a pretty rough time one way and another. What with Uncle Mark, and then Toby . . . she needed someone to help her through it. And as I dare say you'll have gathered, Helen isn't up to much. You'll have to forgive Helen if she seems a trifle—' he waved a hand – 'standoffish? This thing about the house being sold has really got to her.'

'It's got to me, too,' said Jane. 'I don't want us to buy it any more than she does.'

'No, but you're more robust than she is.'

'Oh, am I? Thank you very much!'

'I don't mean physically, you idiot! I meant mentally. Poor old Helen is what I should call . . . emotionally fragile. She was always a bit screwed up, even as a kid; very introverted. Uncle Mark getting killed didn't help any, and then Toby—'

He stopped, abruptly, as if conscious of having said more than intended.

Toby, thought Jane; he must be the son – the one there was some mystery about. Something not quite right. She would have liked to ask except that it might seem rude, and anyway what did she care? She wasn't interested in the Medd-Halls and their family history.

'I guess,' said Andrew, 'the prospect of being turfed out is just the last straw. So if she comes across as not particularly friendly, you'll understand why. It's nothing against you personally.'

'Hardly could be, could it?' said Jane. 'After all, if we don't buy, someone else will.'

'Not necessarily. Not many people have the cash to spare, these days; not for buying old houses that need half a million quids' worth of work done on them.'

'It can't be as much as all that.' Jane said it gloomily. If it had really needed half a million pounds' worth of work then Mum and Dad might not be so tempted.

'Oh, don't be deceived by appearances! This place hasn't been touched since the turn of the century.'

'Unfortunately,' said Jane, 'my dad's a builder. He finds this kind of thing a challenge.'

'All the same . . . not wishing to patronize, but I suppose he does know what he's doing?'

Jane sighed. 'I expect so. He's been at it a long time.'

Andrew was silent a while. Jane stared glumly out of the window at the Downs unfolding in the distance. Beautiful, yes; but not where she belonged!

Andrew, abruptly, swung the wheel and the Downs were left behind.

'They'll keep up the hunting and hacking, I presume?'

'No!' Jane almost squawked in her indignation. How could he possibly think so?

Andrew glanced at her, swiftly, and then looked away. He seemed surprised. A slight frown creased his forehead.

'How could they?' said Jane. 'When they don't know a thing about horses?'

'It's the only part of the business that's viable,' muttered Andrew. 'It's what Shallaford is known for.'

'Then it'll just have to get known for something else, won't it?'

Andrew made no comment.

'If you're anti-bloodsports,' said Jane, 'I should have thought you'd be glad.'

'I'm not thinking of me.'

'No, nor of the foxes!'

'I was thinking of your mum and dad.'

'They can take care of themselves.'

'Can they?' Andrew had pulled to a halt at some traffic lights. He turned to look at her; solemn, for once. 'Far be it from me to try and throw any spanners in the works, but Jane, I'll make no secret of the fact . . . my aunt is pretty desperate. To say she's strapped for cash would be an understatement. I'm not saying she'd be unscrupulous, exactly, but I wouldn't like to see your folks taken for a ride. That's all.'

'I'm sure they won't be,' said Jane; but she thought, all the same, that it might be as well to warn them. Dad might know all there was to know about old properties, but he didn't know the first thing about running a guest house, and neither did Mum. She couldn't bear to see them lose all their money. Going back to the old way of life, nothing but constant worry and struggle, would just about kill them.

'Look, forget I said anything.' Andrew sent the horsebox jolting forward as the lights changed. 'It's no business of mine; I ought to keep my big mouth shut. I've no reason to suppose your parents don't know what they're doing – and anyway, when push comes to shove my loyalties have to lie with my aunt. This is Lewes, incidentally. In just a few seconds, on your left – over there!' He pointed. 'You'll see the place she's thinking of buying if your folks cough up . . . a bit of a come-down after Shallaford, don't you think?'

Jane looked, and saw a pretty pink-washed house – Georgian, she thought, with her dad's eye for quality – standing back off the road behind iron railings. It was the sort of house her dad had dreamed of, back in the old days, the pre-pools-win days, when he couldn't even have afforded the deposit.

'Poor woman,' said Jane. 'My heart bleeds for her.'

'Yes, well, of course—' Andrew gave a little laugh; not quite easy – 'everything is relative. I appreciate that.'

She wondered if he really did.

Fortunately – she supposed it was fortunate: she wouldn't have liked to upset Mum or Dad, though she didn't care tuppence for Lady Medd-Hall – the horsey crew from Shallaford were too busy haw-haw-hawing to one another to notice Jane amongst the crowd of demonstrators. Andrew collected her afterwards – in the Shallaford Land Rover, this time – and no-one was any the wiser.

Mum, rather too eager, greeted her with, 'Had a good time?' and for a moment she was tempted to blurt it out – 'I've had a good demo!' – but managed without too much of a struggle to restrain herself. Mum couldn't help being conventional and regarding every halfway passable young man as a possible boyfriend. (Sean, with his Irish accent and his earring, hadn't been even halfway passable. Sean had worried Mum. She had breathed a sigh of relief when he had gone back to Ireland.)

'Where did you go?' said Mum. 'Up on the Downs?'

'Round and about,' said Jane.

At lunch they had to suffer Helen's brooding presence, but at least the hunting party weren't back yet. Lady Medd-Hall spent half the meal discussing with Andrew whether the going would be good and whether they would be likely to have made a kill: Mum spent half the meal nervously treading on Jane's foot. Funny how she was expected to consider other people's sensitivities all the time, thought Jane, but nobody was expected to consider hers, though to be fair to Andrew he did direct one or two agonized glances in her direction.

Before dinner, Jane telephoned Lynn. She used the upstairs telephone, set in its own little alcove off the main corridor: it was more private than the one in the guests' sitting room, where Mum and Dad were sitting.

'Lynn?' she said. 'It's me.'

'Jane! How are you doing? Did you go on the demo?'

'You bet!'

'What was it like?'

'OK; not bad. There was quite a good turn-out. Listen, when are you going to come down here and keep me company?'

'When do you suggest?'

'Mm . . . Wednesday? For a couple of days?'

The horsey crew would be gone by then and there would only be Jane and her mum and dad. Mum had been doubtful, at first, when Jane had begged that Lynn might come and spend some time with them; she had only given in because she was feeling guilty at dragging Jane away from Highfield and all her friends.

'But you must behave yourselves, Jane,' she'd said. 'You must promise me.'

'We'll behave,' Jane had said. 'We're not barbarians. What do you think we're going to do? Drop all our Hs and eat peas with our fingers?'

Of course Mum hadn't meant that at all, she'd meant 'None of your animal rights nonsense'. That was why it was best to wait till the horsey lot had gone. Not so much provocation.

In the middle of her telephone conversation with Lynn, the upstairs lights suddenly went out.

'Oh, boy!' said Jane. 'That's all we need!'

'What's that?' said Lynn.

'Darkness has descended . . . all the lights have gone.'

'Ugh! Spooky!'

It was, rather. The whole length of the corridor was in almost total blackness, apart from a small yellow pool filtering up from the hall below.

'Weird,' said Jane.

'Is it a power cut?'

'No, I think it must be a fuse. It's OK downstairs.'

'Sounds dodgy to me. Faulty wiring . . . you could go up in smoke.'

'I'd better go and tell them. See you Wednesday!'

'There's been a fuse,' announced Jane, meeting Lady Medd-Hall coming out of the dining room. 'All the upstairs lights have gone out.'

'All of them?' Lady Medd-Hall peered distractedly up the stairs. 'How very extraordinary! I'll get Helen to take a look. Would you care for a candle? Let me fetch you a candle!'

Lady Medd-Hall turned and plunged back into the dining room, re-emerging at the gallop with a white wax candle in a brass candlestick.

'There! You'll be all right now. I always keep some in for emergencies.'

Jane walked back up the stairs with her candle, feeling like something out of a horror movie. Any minute now, a ghostly hand would appear from the shadows, and ghostly fingers would close about her throat . . .

'What's going on?' said Andrew.

Jane jumped, and the flame of her candle flickered and almost went out.

'Don't do that!' said Jane. 'I thought for a moment you were a ghostly hand coming to strangle me.'

'Why? Are we playing Murder? What's happened to the lights?'

'They've gone out,' said Jane. Nothing like stating the obvious.

'Oh, God!' Andrew groaned. 'I'll bet that's Helen mucking about.'

Andrew went on down the stairs, leaving Jane to make her way to her bedroom. She set the candle on the bedside table and groped in the recesses of her wardrobe for her one good pair of trousers. She wondered if perhaps she ought to ask Mum to drive her into Lewes at some stage so that she could buy something else to wear. Not a dress; she drew the line at a dress. But maybe some more trousers and tops. Nothing too ostentatious, it wouldn't be fair on Lynn. In any case—

She stopped. A strange noise was coming down the chimney. A strange burbling sound, like a—

Like a voice.

Jane froze, one leg in and one leg out of her trousers. She strained her ears. Was it a voice?

The burble slowly increased in volume, small balloons of sound swelling and receding as they echoed down the chimney.

It *was* a voice! But a voice that spoke from a long way off – from the end of a tunnel or underwater. Too muffled, and curiously wavy, for any actual words to be deciphered.

Jane zipped up her trousers and ran for the door. As she ran, in her haste, she bumped into the table and knocked over the candle, which promptly went out, leaving her in darkness.

She groped, blindly, for the doorhandle: the door refused to budge. She tried again, twisting fiercely at the handle and yanking. Still it wouldn't budge. Furious, trying not to panic, she beat with both fists on the door panel.

'If there's anybody there will they please let me out!'

If there was anybody there, they obviously had no intention of letting her out: the door remained tight shut. Meanwhile, behind her, the voice burbled on. Amongst the burbles she thought, but could not be certain, that she caught her name.

'Jaaaaane, Jaaaaane . . .'

I'm going to get you, Jane.

Frenziedly, she wrenched yet again at the doorhandle. This time the door flew open. She dived through it, two at a time, down the stairs to the guests' sitting room, where her mum and dad were watching television.

'Quick!' Jane beckoned at them frantically. 'Come and hear!'

'Hear what?' Her dad spoke without taking his eyes off the television.

'Upstairs in my bedroom . . . hurry!'

Jane tore off, with Mum and Dad following. The lights had come back on – a fact she scarcely registered at the time. She flung open the door of her room.

'Listen! Up the chimney!'

There was a silence.

'What's up the chimney?'

'A voice—' Jane faltered. She saw her parents

61

exchange glances. 'Dad,' she said, 'there was! I'm not making it up! I heard it!'

'I can't hear anything,' said her dad.

Nor could Jane, now.

'Maybe it was a bird, or something,' said her mum.

'It wasn't a bird! It was a voice. Mum, I'm telling you!' Jane fell to her knees in the hearth, vainly endeavouring to peer into the darkness.

'Let me get the torch.' Dad sounded resigned: Jane at her tricks again. They thought it was all a big display.

'You're not usually the nervous type,' said Mum.

'I'm not nervous – and I'm not imagining things! It was a voice, I heard it! Mum, there's something spooky about this place. I wish you wouldn't buy it!'

'Now, then, Jane, don't start that! If you think you're going to put us off by behaving like some spoilt child—'

'I'm not behaving like some spoilt child! I'm telling you, *I heard a voice!*'

'You mean, you heard something that sounded like a voice.' Dad had come back, with his torch. He stooped, and shone it up the chimney. 'Go on, then! Have a look. What can you see?'

Jane had to admit that she couldn't see anything.

'Well, there you are. It was probably a bird, like your mum said. You have to remember, you're in the country, now. Things are going to sound different. Just pull yourself together. I can't help feeling—' Dad looked at her, sternly – 'that this is all a bit of a try-on.'

'Dad, I'm not that stupid!'

'Aren't you?' said her dad. 'I'm beginning to wonder.'

'Come down and have a drink, lovey.' Her mum slipped an arm about Jane's shoulders. 'That'll settle you.'

Jane pursed her lips. They were treating her like an idiot.

'Best bring your key,' said Dad, removing it from the outside of the door. 'I know it's not like a proper hotel, but better safe than sorry.'

'Yes, and that's another thing!' said Jane. 'Someone locked me in! The first time I tried to open the door I couldn't get out!'

'Now, look,' said Dad. He fixed her with a firm eye. 'Just stop this, will you? Nobody locked you in! This is an old house.' He rattled her doorhandle. 'The lock needs fixing, that's all. No mystery about it. No call for all this hysteria.'

'It isn't like you, Jane,' said Mum.

Rebellious, yet subdued, Jane allowed herself to be piloted down the stairs and bought a sherry at the bar. She didn't even like sherry, but Mum insisted.

'It'll settle your nerves.'

At least she had the tact, to say it out of Andrew's hearing.

They sat up late that night, watching an old movie on television. The horsey set (who had been obnoxiously exultant over dinner) crashed out early, leaving only Jane and her mum and dad. The house was still and silent as they crossed the main hall;

there were no lights shining under the doors marked
'Private', nor under any of the bedrooms in the long
corridor.

'Night, night, Janey.' Jane's mum dropped a kiss
on her forehead. 'Sleep tight! Try not to have any
more nightmares.'

Jane opened her bedroom door and switched on
the light.

'Ugh!'

She rocketed backwards with a screech, almost
bumping into her dad as he came up the stairs.

'For crying out loud! What is it now?'

'Look—'

Irritably, her dad pushed past her. Jane pointed
with quivering finger across the room: there in the
grate, half covered in soot, lay a dead pigeon.

'Well, that's your answer, isn't it?' said her dad.
'All this nonsense about voices! Your mum was
right; she said it was most probably a bird.'

'What are we going to do with it?' whispered Jane.

'Get us something to put it in. A bag, or something.'

Mum scuttled off obediently to find one. Jane
crouched on the hearth, gazing down sadly at the
dead pigeon. Unlike its scruffy grey cousins in
Shepherd's Bush, this one had been plump with
palest brown plumage. Its once beautiful head lolled
at an angle, the round bright eyes already glazed.

Jane stretched out a finger and gently stroked it.

'Poor pigeon,' she murmured.

'Poor pigeon be blowed! The things are vermin.'

Jane's mum appeared with a carrier-bag. Jane
turned her head, unwilling to watch as her dad
scooped the pigeon into it.

'We'll get rid of it tomorrow. I'll dump it outside for now.'

A tremor ran through Jane.

'Poor Janey!' Mum put an arm round her. 'Be brave! I know it's not very nice, but at least it's solved the riddle.'

It might have solved it for Mum: it hadn't solved it for Jane. There had been a voice; she knew that there had.

4

'And how did Jane sleep last night?' Lady Medd-Hall had discarded her pink nylon smock for an identical one in blue. She beamed brightly at Jane across the breakfast table. 'No more horrid radios keeping you awake?'

Jane shook her head, casting a glance at Helen as she did so, but Helen had her nose buried in a hi-fi magazine (charming manners, these gentlefolk) and showed no signs of guilt, though the radio obviously must have been her.

'Thank goodness for that! I don't like the thought of my guests having cause for complaint.'

'Oh, this one'll always find something to complain about.' Dad jerked his thumb in Jane's direction. 'If it's not phantom radios, it's voices down the chimney.'

'My dear!'

'Neil! Don't,' implored Mum.

'Voices down the chimney!' Patsy sniggered. 'That's a new one!'

'*A* voice,' said Jane. She knew what Dad's game was. He was trying to make her look foolish; trying to shame her into admitting it had all

66

been a take-on. Well, she wasn't going to admit it because it hadn't been.

Needless to say, everyone except Helen was gawping at her; Andrew with a frown on his face.

'Do tell more!' begged Mrs Bland. 'This sounds most intriguing!'

'Not really,' said Dad. 'All it turned out to be was a dead pigeon. We've left it outside, by the way. We didn't quite know what else to do with it.'

'Oh, that's all right!' Lady Medd-Hall sounded positively cheerful. 'We can cope with dead pigeons. I'm sorry it had to choose Jane's chimney though. Poor Jane! You're having rather an unfortunate time of it, aren't you?'

'Don't worry,' said Dad. 'She thrives on it. Sh—'

'Excuse me.' Helen stood up, abruptly, and left the room. Andrew's eyes followed her; he seemed concerned. Nobody else, including her mother, took the slightest bit of notice. It was almost, thought Jane, as if Helen didn't exist.

'She likes a bit of melodrama,' said Dad.

'Nevertheless,' said Lady Medd-Hall, 'one would rather it hadn't occurred. I do assure you that it is most unusual. We do not have Goings On at Shallaford. Do we?'

She turned as usual to Andrew for confirmation. Andrew dipped his head.

'Absolutely not. If anyone is looking for excitement—' he half closed an eye at Jane as he spoke – 'Shallaford is not the place for them.'

'Quite. We exist in our own little vacuum. Nothing disturbs the even tenor of our ways.'

'Except,' said Andrew, 'when dead pigeons come raining down the chimney.'

'I thought, you know, that we had had those chimneys netted?'

Andrew shrugged. 'I guess netting wears out the same as everything else.'

'Please don't worry about it,' said Mum.

'Well, but I do feel so sorry for poor Jane! Especially as she is not a meat-eater, and no doubt this kind of thing is rather upsetting. I always feel,' said Lady Medd-Hall, in musing tones, 'that vegetarians are probably rather more sensitive than the rest of us.'

'Don't you believe it,' said Dad. 'Tough as old boots, this one . . . thinks nothing of kicking policemen's teeth down their throats for them.'

'How very brave!' said Lady Medd-Hall. 'I do so envy people who have the courage to stand up for their principles. A frightful nuisance, of course; but somehow rather admirable. Now, what are everyone's plans for today? I know you four are going for a hack. How about you, Mrs Lawlor, dear? What are you up to?'

Mum said that she and Dad had thought of going for a drive.

'That's right; get out and see the countryside. How about Jane? Is she going to see the countryside?'

Jane supposed, unless she fugged indoors and read a book, that she didn't have much alternative.

'Jane's coming for a walk with me,' said Andrew. 'Yes?'

Jane brightened.

'Oh!' wailed Patsy. 'I thought you were coming for a hack?'

'*I* thought you were going for a hack,' said Lady Medd-Hall.

'Can't,' said Andrew. 'Who could I ride?'

'Trumpeter?'

'He's lame; I looked at him. And the others need a rest. So!' He smiled his lopsided smile at Jane. 'You and me shall go walkies. Shall we?'

'I'm so glad,' whispered Jane's mum as they went upstairs after breakfast, 'that you're getting on with Andrew. He really is a very nice boy.'

So different from the yobs you normally knock about with. Unfortunately, Jane had to admit it, Andrew had rather more social graces than Sean had had. Rough and ready, that was Sean. But then, she thought angrily – was she going soft? – Andrew had had advantages that Sean had never dreamed of. It was an unfair comparison; anyone could have social graces if they had been brought up in the lap of luxury.

Andrew was waiting for her downstairs in the hall.

'I trust you're feeling energetic, because when I say walk I do mean walk.'

'I can walk!' said Jane. Hadn't she tramped the streets for hours on end, distributing leaflets, going on demos? He needn't think that just because she was a townie she was soft.

As they went through the front door, the two dogs came bounding up.

'Down!' roared Andrew.

They cowered, immediately.

'It's all right,' said Jane. 'I like dogs. Can we take them with us?'

'No!' Helen had appeared, round the side of the house. She called the dogs to her, guarding them jealously, an arm round each, her face

69

contorted. 'They're coming with me.'

Jane bit her lip. She could appreciate that Helen resented her, but why did she have to be so unpleasant all the time? Jane had only wanted to take them for a walk. It wasn't some ploy to steal their affections.

'Sorry,' said Jane. She found that she was feeling quite hurt. She wasn't as a rule so sensitive; maybe it was because it was the dogs. She had wanted a dog of her own ever since she could remember. 'I didn't realize you were taking them.'

Helen muttered something in her usual dulcet tones – even her voice was ugly: it sounded like something scraped from the bottom of a barrel – and strode off in her ungainly fashion across the lawn, the dogs gambolling behind her. Jane and Andrew turned in the opposite direction.

'Accept my apologies,' murmured Andrew. 'I'm afraid she's getting a bit—'

Jane waited.

'A bit what?'

'I was going to say a bit paranoid, but that's a sensitive word round here. Just forget I ever mentioned it.'

'Why?'

Suddenly, he was striding ahead of her. Jane did a little skip to catch up.

'Why should I forget it?' she said.

'Because I ask you to?'

Jane marched for a while in silence, a frown creasing her forehead.

'Are you seriously saying she's—' She suppressed the first word which came to mind. You didn't go

70

round calling people loopy. 'Are you seriously saying she's . . . mentally disturbed?'

'No!' He swung round to face her. 'That's not what I'm saying at all.'

'Then what—'

'Toby,' he muttered. 'Not Helen.'

Toby again.

'Who is this Toby?' said Jane.

'Her brother. He's – confined. In an institution; just down the road from here. She still visits him regularly. They were – very close, him and Helen. My aunt doesn't like to talk about it, so please! Don't mention any of this to her. When I said paranoid, it was just—' he flicked a lock of hair out of his eyes – 'just one of those stupid expressions one uses without thinking. All I actually meant was . . . I know Helen's behaving atrociously and I'm sorry about that, but I can understand what's driving her. She's clinging to the house as the one last stable factor in her life.'

'She doesn't have to take it out on me!'

'Jane, she's a very unhappy person. Unhappiness can unbalance people; it's not her fault. If you could just possibly try to pretend that it's not happening—'

'OK.' Jane hunched a shoulder. 'I'm thick-skinned.'

'Are you?' He glanced at her. 'You're having a pretty rough ride here, aren't you?'

'I didn't expect to enjoy myself.'

'No, and I don't suppose you expected dead pigeons to come dropping down the chimney, either. Tell me—' Andrew hesitated. 'You didn't manage to – get a close look at this pigeon?'

'I couldn't very well avoid it,' said Jane.

'It wasn't . . . a brown and white one, by any chance?'

'Yes. Light brown – sort of pinky.'

Slowly, Andrew nodded.

'Why? It wasn't a pet one, was it?'

'Not a pet one, exactly; I don't think you have pet pigeons. But it was sort of . . . semi-tame. It used to come to you, if you had food. We called it Charlie. It was always about. I thought it hadn't been around for a day or two.'

'How do they get to fall down chimneys?' said Jane.

'I don't know.' His tone was sombre. 'It's a puzzle, isn't it?'

A lot of things round here were a puzzle, thought Jane.

'What was all this about voices, by the way?'

'A voice.'

'A voice. What was that all about?'

'Oh, nothing,' said Jane. 'You'll only think I'm barmy.'

'I won't. I promise!'

'How can you promise when you haven't heard what it is?'

'Try me!'

'Well . . . it was this voice.' Jane said it reluctantly. Why couldn't Dad have kept his mouth shut? 'Down the chimney.'

'Saying what?'

'It didn't actually *say* anything. Not that I could make out.'

'So what did it sound like?'

'Sort of . . . boomy. And wavy.' Jane imitated it, as best she could.

'Like a tape being played at half-speed.'

'Yes, or like someone talking underwater. Not in the least bit like a bird.'

'Hardly.'

Well, at least he hadn't dismissed it as hysteria. Yet.

Casually, she said, 'So what would your guess be?'

'Oh! Well – you know. Old houses.' He sounded uncomfortable. 'One does tend to hear the odd noise every now and again.'

'Odd noises like voices?'

If he tries to tell me it was an owl, she thought, I shall scream.

'I suppose—' he hesitated – 'it could have been Helen messing with her hi-fi again?'

'What, down the chimney?'

'No, I suppose not – though you'd be surprised how sound carries. It's something you'll have to get used to if you're going to take up residence here.'

'*If*,' said Jane.

She hadn't altogether given up hope that this fortnight might persuade her parents of their folly. Who needed the hassle of a guest house at their stage of life? All right, so forty wasn't exactly old, but it wasn't young, either. Why couldn't they be content with moving to a better house in a better area and developing some hobbies? Dad had his golf and his beloved hi-fi; that would keep him going. Mum could take up voluntary work, or something. Something with people. She'd like that.

'I'm going to have another go at them,' said Jane. 'Tell them what you said about all the work that needs doing.'

'Oh, now, look! I didn't mean to put them off.

I shouldn't have said all that stuff the other day. I mean, your dad's a builder, he's not going to let himself be diddled.'

'He won't be diddled,' said Jane, 'but he might bite off more than he can chew.'

'Well, but that's nothing to do with me; OK? I ought to learn to button my lip.'

'Don't worry,' said Jane. 'I won't drop you in it.'

On her way back upstairs before lunch, she bumped into Helen coming along the passage. Helen gave a start when she saw Jane; almost as if she had been caught doing something she shouldn't.

'Did you enjoy your walk?' she said.

It was obviously an effort for her; her cheeks fired up as she said it.

'Yes, thank you,' said Jane. 'Did you enjoy yours?'

'Yes. Yes, thank you.'

'And the dogs?' called Jane, as Helen shot off down the stairs.

'And the dogs. Yes!'

Where had she come from? wondered Jane. She had been walking along the passage in quite the opposite direction from her own room. The Medd-Halls slept on the next floor, which was reached via the stairs that ran up past the bathroom. At this end, beyond the main staircase, there were only Jane's room and her parents', and some kind of a cupboard, or what she took to be a cupboard. She tried the handle, but it was locked. Maybe that was where Helen had been; maybe she kept some of her hi-fi stuff in there. But in that case, why the guilty expression? Just Helen, she supposed. As Andrew had said, unhappiness could unbalance people.

74

He waylaid her as she made her way down to lunch.

'Jane!' He spoke urgently, in a low voice. 'I've been thinking . . . what we were talking about this morning. If anything else – peculiar – happens, you will let me know, won't you?'

'Well – yes. OK. But—'

'No buts! Promise.'

'All right,' said Jane. 'I promise.'

She tensed herself that evening, when she went up to bed, but no dead pigeons lay awaiting her in the grate, no voices came booming down the chimney, no faces peered in at the window. She slept soundly for almost the first time since coming to Shallaford.

The following morning the horsey set departed and Mum drove Jane into Lewes to buy some clothes before meeting Lynn at the station. Mum was only too happy for Jane to buy clothes, especially as (she hinted) there wouldn't be the same sort of way-out gear in Lewes as there was in London. In fact there was if Jane had wanted it, but perhaps for a change, she thought, she would go for a more classical look. Nothing to do with Andrew, which was what Mum also hinted. (Mum was so *unsubtle*.)

Jane had been looking forward to being with Lynn again. Perhaps she had almost looked forward to it too much, so that it was bound to have been a disappointment. She hadn't realized how out of place Lynn would seem at Shallaford. Of course, Jane and her mum and dad were also out of place, which was what Jane had prophesied right at the beginning, but Mum was so determined to be happy that she didn't even notice, and Dad was quite impervious. Even Jane, who had arrived full of disgruntlement, determined to loathe everything about the place, was finding it not quite as bad as she had feared.

Lynn didn't even give it a chance.

'God!' she said, as she and Jane went to bed that night. (At Jane's special request they were sharing a bedroom, as they had when they were much younger and had stayed overnight at each other's houses.) 'This is grotesque! That frightful woman!'

'Lady Medd-Hall?' Jane giggled. 'I call her Lady Lump!'

'Grand! Splendid! Super!' Lynn managed to sound uncannily like her. 'Daft old bag!'

'She's all right,' said Jane, 'when you get used to her.'

'Yeah? And what about that snotty-nosed daughter? Who does she think she is? Queen of bleeding England?'

'Helen is a bit of a pain,' agreed Jane. 'But she can't help it. Her dad got killed in an accident and her brother's got something wrong with him. I think he might be schizophrenic, or something. He has to live in an institution.'

'Tough!' said Lynn. 'It still doesn't stop her needing a good kick up the backside. And as for that ponce Andrew—'

Jane stiffened.

'He could do with stuffing and putting under glass!'

'As a matter of actual fact,' said Jane, 'Andrew is OK.'

'OK? He's a creep!'

Jane was nettled. What right had Lynn to accept an invitation at someone else's expense (Mum and Dad were paying for her) and start slagging everybody off before she had even been in the place five minutes?

'What do you know about it?' she said. 'You only just got here.'

'Oh! I see.' Lynn curled her lip. 'It's like that, is it?'

'Like what?'

'You've gone and fallen for him just because he's got a pretty face.'

'I have not gone and fallen for him!' Jane refuted it, angrily. 'I simply said he was OK.'

'What, with a voice like that? It sounds like a strangulated hernia!'

'People—' Jane cut in quickly before Lynn could start taking off Andrew – 'can't help the way they talk. If it hadn't been for him I couldn't have got to the demo. Dad refused to take me. It was Andrew who drove me there.'

'Big deal!'

'Well, it was,' said Jane, 'when you consider that this place is Bloodsports Hall.'

'God, I don't know how you stand it!'

'I haven't got much option, have I?'

'Poor little rich girl!' mocked Lynn. 'Mummy and Daddy have gone up in the world and she has to trail along at their coat-tails!'

'Well, what else could I have done?'

'You didn't have to come with them, did you? You could always have stayed behind.'

'What, over Christmas?'

'Why not? I could have come round and we could

have made whoopee all by ourselves.'

Jane and Lynn's friendship had not been without its ups and downs over the years. They were both strong characters and by no means always saw eye to eye, but Jane had never felt quite as estranged from Lynn as she did that night. She had been looking forward to exchanging confidences as they lay in bed in the dark. It was what they would have done in the old days. Now she hesitated. Lynn-in-Shepherd's-Bush would have thrilled to the tales of strange happenings. She would have taken them seriously and never doubted for a minute but that they had actually occurred. Lynn-at-Shallaford was an unknown quantity. She seemed suddenly a different person – brash and hard; no trace of the old bubbling irreverent Lynn who could pull Jane's leg and make her laugh.

'I must tell you, by the way,' said Lynn, settling herself in bed, 'that gear you bought today is dead naff.'

'Oh. Really,' said Jane.

'Yeah, really,' said Lynn.

'Good thing you told me . . . I mightn't have realized, otherwise.'

'Well, come on, you don't have to get on your high horse! What's the matter with you? Can't you take a bit of friendly advice any more?'

'That wasn't friendly advice.' Jane mumbled it into the pillow. 'That was just being bitchy.'

'Don't you come that sexist stuff with me! You've changed since you came into money. Did you know that? Oy!' Lynn leaned across and poked at Jane's shoulder. 'You! I said you've changed.'

'I'm not the only one,' muttered Jane.

She didn't believe it was her that had changed; or if she had, then Lynn had, too. She wished now that she had never told Lynn about Mum and Dad winning the pools. Mum had warned her at the time, but she hadn't listened. She had thought that nothing would ever come between her and Lynn.

The next two days were not a success. Jane developed the first symptoms of a cold, which made her prickly and short-tempered. Lynn was all sweetness and light in public – Lynn could have nice manners, when she wanted – and all carping criticism alone with Jane at night. Lady Medd-Hall was a buffoon, Helen was a snob, Jane's mum was servile, Jane's dad didn't seem to realize that they were all laughing at him behind his back, Andrew—

Andrew, she had grudgingly conceded, after he had driven them over to Brighton and they had all spent the morning there, 'could have been worse'. High praise, coming from Lynn in her present mood.

By Friday afternoon, when she was due to return home, Jane had the feeling they were both secretly relieved that it had come to an end.

It was Andrew who drove Lynn in to Lewes to catch her train. Mum had been going to do it, but Andrew said he had business to conduct there anyway and might as well kill two birds with one stone, which suited Mum. She had never been fond of Lynn. Jane, at the last moment, decided against going with them. Her head was aching, her nose stuffed up; why should she bother to stir herself? Lynn had been perfectly foul ever since she got there.

Of course, the minute they had left she wished she had gone with them. It was true that Lynn had behaved badly, but then Jane hadn't behaved so terribly well herself when she had first arrived. (She could still remember saying 'Hi' to Lady Medd-Hall in as obnoxious a manner as possible.) And then it couldn't be much fun for Lynn, still being poor and living in rotten crumbling rooms in a house that should have been pulled down centuries ago while her best friend flaunted herself in new clothes (even if they were dead naff) and had parents who were thinking of handing over a cool half million for a place in the country. She ought to have made allowances. She ought at least to have accompanied Lynn to the station and said a proper goodbye. She made up her mind that she would telephone Lynn that same evening.

The house was empty, apart from Helen doing things with bits of wire in the hall. Lady Medd-Hall was in the village, Mum and Dad had taken the opportunity to drive over to Eastbourne to visit friends. Jane decided she might as well go and lie down for a couple of hours before dinner.

Helen, very briefly, glanced up as she passed but didn't say anything; she hardly ever did. Jane leaned out over the banisters.

'I'll be in my room if anyone wants me.'

Helen barely even grunted an acknowledgement.

'Oh, well! Suit yourself,' thought Jane.

Jane was tucked up in bed, dozing, when a tap at the door awoke her. She shot up the bed, immediately alert.

'Yes?'

'There's someone on the telephone for you.'

It was Helen's voice. Jane padded across to the door.

80

'Who is it?'

'I think it's your friend,' said Helen. 'The one that was here.'

'Lynn?'

'I think so.'

Jane brightened. Maybe Lynn, too, had been having last-minute regrets.

'Do you want me to transfer it for you?'

'Yes. Please,' said Jane. Really, Helen was being almost civil for once.

The call came through on the upstairs extension. Jane picked up the receiver.

'Hello? Lynn?'

There was a silence. Not the silence of a line that has gone dead; the sort of silence where you can tell that there is someone there. Someone listening, but not speaking.

'Lynn?' said Jane. 'Is that you?'

The someone who was listening started to breathe down the telephone. Fingers of fear crept over Jane's flesh.

'Who is that?' she said.

The breather said nothing; just went on breathing, louder, deeper, increasing in intensity until it was almost slavering, like some large animal salivating over its prey.

'Lynn, if that's you, you're a moron!' screamed Jane.

She crashed the receiver on to its rest and went racing down the stairs to the hall. Helen was still there, messing with her wires; she was standing right next to the telephone.

'Did you say that was Lynn calling me?' said Jane.

Helen looked at her for a moment, then dropped her eyes. 'I thought it was.'

'Where was she supposed to be calling from?'

'I don't know. She didn't say.'

Helen picked up her tools and walked across the hall to one of the doors marked 'Private'. There she stopped and turned.

'Are you feeling all right?' she said. 'Would you like me to get you a glass of hot milk?'

'No, thank you!' snapped Jane. 'I don't drink food that's meant for calves.'

Helen raised her eyebrows and without another word disappeared through the door. OK, thought Jane, so now it's me being rude to her. But Helen had been listening in, she was almost sure of it. Either listening in, or—

Jane moved across to the telephone. She studied it a moment, frowning, then walked back up the stairs, uneasily, to her bedroom. Just how un-balanced *was* Helen?

That evening, Jane telephoned Lynn.

'Did you try ringing me earlier, from Lewes?' she said.

'No.' Lynn sounded part truculent, part on the defensive. 'Should I have done?'

'I just thought you might,' said Jane.

She knew that Lynn wasn't a liar, and in any case, no matter how peeved she was she wouldn't have played a stupid trick like that, but she asked Andrew all the same.

'Lynn?' he said. 'No, I was with her right up until she got on the train. Why?' He looked at Jane, searchingly. 'Is anything wrong? Jane? You promised to tell me!'

Haltingly, she did so. Andrew listened in silence.

'I suppose it's always possible there was a telephone on the train . . . it could just have been Lynn having a joke.'

'I suppose it could have been,' said Jane, but she only said it to keep him happy. She didn't believe it, and she knew that Andrew didn't, either.

5

'How are you feeling this morning?' Andrew stood waiting at the top of the stairs as Jane went down to breakfast. 'Cold any better?'

'Loads, thanks.'

'Good! I take it—' he lowered his voice – 'you had an undisturbed night? Nothing . . . untoward occurred?'

'Well, if it did, I slept right through it.'

'So you're feeling refreshed?'

'I'm feeling fine!'

'Strong enough to come for a ride? Do you ride?'

Dubiously, Jane said, 'I once sat on a donkey on the beach.'

'Oh, we can do better than donkeys! How about it? Want to give it a go?'

'Why not?' said Jane. 'Try anything once!'

Mum, predictably, was delighted when Jane told her.

'You see? There *are* things to do in the country! There might not be wild rave-ups—'

Mum was referring to the fact that today was New Year's Eve. Last New Year's Eve Jane had gone to a party with Lynn and come giggling home by cab at one o'clock in the morning. This year, Lynn was going to a party by herself and Jane wasn't going anywhere. Nothing was happening at sleepy Shallaford because the Lawlors were the only people there and Lady Medd-Hall didn't really cater for guests in the after-Christmas period.

'Of course we'll stay up and see the New Year in,' had said Jane's dad; but where was the fun of staying up with parents? Andrew was going to a party. He had expressed regret that he couldn't invite Jane – 'But it's all the hunting set. You wouldn't like it. I can't very well get out of it, unfortunately . . . good relations and all that.'

Was Jane imagining it, or would he really have preferred to stay behind and see the New Year in with her, at Shallaford?

'Imagine,' said Mum, coaxingly, 'if we came to live in the country you could have a horse of your own.'

'What, and join the green welly brigade? No, thank you!'

'Jane, riding in the country isn't like it is in town . . . quite ordinary people have horses in the country. Even quite poor people.'

'Even people living on income support.'

'Oh, now, Jane—'

'Mum, stop nagging at me! I don't *want* to come and live in the country.'

Mum sighed. 'I'd hoped you were getting used to the idea.'

'Well, I'm not! And it won't be fair if you make me!'

Jane knew that she had upset her mum, and perhaps that wasn't fair, either, because Mum was more vulnerable than Dad – Jane and her dad were very much alike: they could both be what her mum called pig-headed – but just because she enjoyed going out with Andrew they needn't jump to the conclusion that she had become reconciled, because she hadn't.

Andrew was in the stables, putting a bridle on a small grey horse.

'This is Tara,' he said. 'You'll be quite safe on her.'

'I'm not scared,' said Jane.

'No, but your parents mightn't like it if you came back with a broken neck . . . here!' He thrust a riding hat at her. 'You'd better put this on.'

Helen arrived, with the two dogs, while Andrew was still tacking up. She seemed to follow him everywhere; almost as if she were spying on him, thought Jane. It occurred to her that perhaps Helen was a little jealous. After all, before Jane had come here she would have had Andrew all to herself.

She leaned against the side of a loosebox, watching as he did up the saddle straps, or whatever they were called. (The girth? Was that what it was?)

'Who are you taking? You can't take Trumpeter, he's still lame.'

'I'm aware of that.' Andrew said it mildly. Jane had noticed that he was always very patient with his tiresome cousin; more patient, if you asked Jane, than she had any right to expect. 'I'd thought of taking Goodfella, or did you want him?'

Helen shook her head.

'I don't want him, but he was out for three hours yesterday. It would be better if you took Sherpa, only don't let him blow himself; Major Harrington's booked him for tomorrow.'

'He's not very likely to blow himself,' said

Andrew, 'considering Jane here is a complete beginner. We shall be doing nothing but walk. We might attempt a bit of a trot,' he murmured, as they finally left the yard, 'but we're certainly not going to go mad.'

'Does she think you don't know what you're doing?' said Jane.

'They're her horses, you see. Well – not hers, exactly; Aunt Elinor's. But Helen's been around them a long time.'

Jane frowned; he was always making excuses for Helen. In her opinion, people could have too many excuses made for them. There came a time when you just had to learn to cope.

'I know what you're thinking,' said Andrew. 'You're thinking I'm too soft with her.'

'Well, but if you keep letting her get away with things—'

'What things?'

She had the feeling he was challenging her. Go on! Say it, if you dare!

'Yesterday,' said Jane, 'that telephone business—'

'What about it?'

'It was her! I'm sure it was!'

'Just because she was the one who put the call through?'

'She was the only other person in the house!'

'It could quite genuinely have come from outside,' said Andrew.

'But she said it was Lynn!'

There was a silence. Andrew bent over to adjust one of his stirrups.

'You're not suggesting,' said Jane, 'that it *was* Lynn?'

87

'Jane, I don't know; I really don't know. All I know is that . . . we've no actual proof that it was Helen.'

'You just don't want to believe that it was Helen!'

'Like you just don't want to believe that it was Lynn.'

'But why should it have been?'

He fell silent again.

'Give me one good reason,' said Jane.

'To pay you out? Get her own back?'

'For what?'

'Money can cause an awful lot of problems,' muttered Andrew.

'If you're trying to say that she's jealous—'

'Wouldn't you be? In her position?'

'No! At least – I might be a bit envious. I wouldn't be *jealous*.'

'Maybe you're a different sort of person. She gave me the impression – oh! I don't know, I'm probably speaking out of turn.'

'Go on!' said Jane. 'She gave you the impression?'

'When I drove her in to Lewes . . . various things she was saying. I got the impression that she . . . reckoned you'd changed. "Jumped-up" was the way she put it.'

'Lynn said I was jumped-up?' Jane was indignant – and hurt, too. It was one thing for Lynn to accuse her to her face; quite another to go round accusing her to outsiders. Especially to Andrew, whom she had originally considered a creep.

'I think perhaps I was to blame.' Andrew said it apologetically. 'I was telling her how it had made all the difference to Christmas, having you here. Someone I could talk to. Someone I could go for walks with. Someone who – speaks the same language.'

Jane's face glowed red hot like a cinder. She was not a girl to blush easily, but she was not much accustomed to compliments. Sean, even with all his Irish blarney, had not had much time for them.

'She seemed to think—' he gave a little laugh; awkward, embarrassed – 'that it was almost a case of class treachery.'

'Oh, honestly!' said Jane, blithely disregarding the fact that a week ago she, too, would have considered it class treachery. 'That sort of attitude went out with the Ark!'

'Well, that's what I thought, but it seems that in the eyes of Lynn you have transgressed . . . *idées au dessus de ta gare!*'

'Pardon?' said Jane.

'Ze ideas above ze station.'

'Oh! *Gare*; station! Yes.' She was anxious that he should know: she had learnt French.

'It's all so asinine,' said Andrew, 'that sort of thing.'

'Yes, it is – and so is making infantile telephone calls! If I thought that was Lynn, I'd – I'd scrag her!'

'You still think it was Helen, don't you?'

'I don't know what I think any more. I'm sick of it! And it couldn't have been Lynn playing all those other stupid tricks.'

'No.' Andrew admitted it, gravely. 'That silly business with the pigeon—'

'And all the other things! Or do you think I was just imagining them?'

He hesitated.

'You do!' said Jane. 'Don't you? You're like Mum and Dad! You think I just made them up.'

'Of course I don't think you made them up. What would be the point of your doing that?'

'According to them, it's me trying to persuade them not to buy the house.'

'They reckon you're that desperate?' Andrew turned, in the saddle. 'You really don't want to come and live here, do you?' He said it as if it were a revelation – as if up until now he had only half believed her.

'I don't want to come and live here,' said Jane, 'but I'm not batty enough to go round making up horror stories just to put them off.'

'I wasn't suggesting that you were.'

'But you still think they didn't really happen!' She flung it at him, boldly. 'You'd rather pretend I'm mad and hysterical than admit you've got a cousin who's off her trolley!'

'Helen is not off her trolley.'

'You said she was paranoid!'

'I said—' he dropped his voice – 'I said that Toby was. I did admit that Helen's slightly . . . eccentric. I told you she wanders about at night and potters with her electronics and stuff. I just don't think it's fair to blame this telephone incident on her when we haven't any proof.'

No, he'd sooner blame it on Lynn. Doubts were already starting in Jane's mind. *Could* it have been Lynn?

'Have you spoken to your mum and dad again yet, by the way? Found out what their intentions are?'

Glumly, Jane shook her head.

'I only ask because – well! To be honest, I'm feeling a bit guilty.'

'*You* are? Why?'

'Trying to put you off the idea, when Aunt Elinor is so desperate to sell. I could kick myself! If the deal falls through, I shall feel it was all my fault.'

'It wouldn't be your fault, it wouldn't be anything to do with you. Nothing you've said's likely to budge them. And anyway, it almost certainly won't fall through. Dad's already talking of getting an architect to draw up plans.'

'Well, for Aunt Elinor's sake I have to say I'm relieved. I'm sorry it's not such good news for you.'

'Or for Helen.'

'Helen's just a spoiled brat.' He spoke, for once, quite sharply. 'Too used to having her own way. Don't you worry about her, she'll survive.'

'What about you?' Jane looked at him, curiously. 'Don't you mind?'

'About Shallaford?' He locked his fingers in his horse's mane, twisting the thick hair. 'I do; of course I do. But I'm a bit more realistic than Helen. For one thing, I haven't always been pampered and cosseted as she and Toby were. For another, I wasn't actually born and bred here. I've never had any . . . expectations. Poor old Toby was brought up to believe he'd inherit both the house and the title. Instead, all he's got is the title – and much use it is to him.'

Jane sat soberly as her horse picked its way on delicate feet round the edge of a boggy patch. (She was fine so long as it didn't do anything unexpected, such as skittering sideways.)

'I suppose—' she said it thoughtfully – 'I suppose

it is a pity the house is going to be messed around with.'

'A pity!' He laughed. 'Tell that to Toby and Helen!'

'Well, yes, I'm sure they'd think it sacrilege—'

'Worse than sacrilege.'

'But Dad will make a good job of it,' said Jane, 'I promise you! He really loves old buildings. He's converted loads of them; he always tries to keep as much of the original as he possibly can. And it's not as if it's really historical, is it? It's not Jacobean, or Elizabethan, or anything. I mean, I know it's a nice house and all that, but you couldn't actually say it was anything special. Architecturally, I mean. It's only Vic – hey!'

Jane broke off in panic as Andrew's horse quite suddenly lit out at the gallop, drawing hers after it like a magnet.

'Hey! Stop!' screeched Jane. She hauled desperately on the reins. Tara, little grey Tara – *you'll be quite safe on her* – obviously had a will of her own. She took not the least notice of Jane and her puny efforts to restrain her. Her head tossed up and she was away. Jane could only cling on frantically, bouncing in the saddle, as they thundered across the ground in pursuit of Andrew. God, let him stop! Please let him stop!

By the time Andrew managed to get his big black hunter under control and come wheeling back towards her, Jane was already slipping sideways.

'Whoa!' Andrew reached out and snatched at Tara's bridle. Tara, obedient, skidded to a halt: Jane, slowly and gracefully, slithered to the ground.

'Jane!' Andrew had dismounted immediately and

was at her side, helping her up. 'God, I'm sorry! Are you all right?'

'Yes,' said Jane, surprised to find herself still whole. 'I'm OK.' A bit unnerved, perhaps, but far too proud to show it.

'This bloody nag! Behaving like a maniac. I knew I should have taken Goodfella. Are you quite sure you're all right?' He looked down at her, obviously concerned. She had the feeling he might almost have put an arm about her if he hadn't been holding a horse's bridle in either hand. 'I'm desperately sorry. What a ghastly thing to happen – and on your first time out! You'll never trust me again.'

'Well, but I'll have to—' Jane laughed, a trifle shakily but in control – 'or I won't be able to get back!'

'It won't happen a second time, I promise you. That's what comes of talking and not paying attention – you can't afford to relax for an instant with this brute. I wouldn't have taken him if Helen hadn't insisted. Still, I can't blame her. The buck stops here, as someone or other once said. Do you want a leg up, or can you manage?'

'I can manage.' She might not be too keen, but it was a matter of principle.

'For heaven's sake, don't mention it to Helen! She'll be convinced I did it on purpose just to spite her.'

'Helen and I,' said Jane, gathering the reins somewhat nervously into her hands, 'are not exactly in the habit of holding conversations. And why should she think you wanted to spite her?'

'Oh – well! You know Helen. She tells me not to let the thing blow itself and then it takes off at the gallop . . . I'm an experienced rider, I'm supposed to know better. It wouldn't have happened with Goodfella; but this nag—' He slapped disdainfully at its flank. Jane tensed. 'Don't worry,' said Andrew. 'He's not playing the same trick twice. You OK? Ready for the off? We'll take it nice and slowly, no more surprises. You did extraordinarily well, by the way. Most beginners would have parted company half a mile back. You've obviously got the makings of a rider.'

Jane glowed. She didn't want to glow – she disapproved of women going all gooey just because a man said nice things to them – but she couldn't stop herself. She could feel her face lighting up like a big happy beacon. Pathetic! How Lynn would sneer. (But she had had enough of Lynn. Even if she did go back to Heathfield they would never be friends again; not real friends, as they had been. Talking about her to Andrew was quite un-forgivable.)

She half expected Helen to be hanging around in the yard when they got back, ready to pounce on the horses and inspect them for signs of blowing, but surprisingly the yard was empty.

'Want to give me a hand putting them away?' said Andrew. 'Or have you had enough?'

'I'm all right.' Jane said it stoutly. 'I'll give you a hand.'

They settled the horses and walked round together to the house. Jane looked into the guests' sitting room to let Mum and Dad know that she was back – 'Enjoy yourself?' said Dad. 'You could have a horse of your own, you know, if we moved to the country.' Now even Dad had started it – and went upstairs to collect her sponge bag and towel to have a wash. As she came out of the bathroom she bumped into Helen.

'Sorry,' said Jane.

Helen mumbled something inaudible, in her usual fashion, and shot up the stairs to the family's private quarters. Jane shrugged her shoulders and continued along the passage. She had only been out of her room for a few minutes and hadn't bothered to lock the door; she also, it seemed, hadn't bothered to shut it properly. Frowning slightly, she pushed it open. In spite of bracing herself, she couldn't quite suppress a shudder of revulsion. There, in the middle of the bed, was another little surprise: a dead rat, bleeding from the mouth.

Jane swallowed. Right; that did it. Helen Medd-Hall, you are not going to scare the pants off me. I do not scare easily. Do you hear me? *I do not scare easily.*

Jane dropped her sponge bag on a chair. Determinedly she approached the thing on her bed. It was large and brown – and definitely dead. She knew that it was dead and that it couldn't possibly do anything to her, but still she couldn't quite nerve herself to pick it up even with her towel. In the end, she gathered up the entire quilt and carried it downstairs with her. Everyone, including Helen, had already gone into the dining room. Lady Medd-Hall was in the act of serving lunch as Jane marched through the door.

'Jane, what on earth—' began her mum.

'I thought you'd like to see what I've found this time.' Jane laid the quilt on the floor, with a flourish. Mum screamed, Lady Medd-Hall dropped a serving spoon. Andrew and Helen, both on the far side of the table, craned to see. One of the dogs, meanwhile, had leapt forward, seized the rat in its jaws and gone chasing off with it into the hall.

'Stop him!' yelled Helen. It was the most animated Jane had ever heard her. 'It could be poisoned!'

Helen shot out after the dog. The other dog, plus Andrew, shot after her.

'Jane, for heaven's sake!' bawled her dad. 'What was the idea of that?'

'Don't ask me,' said Jane. 'It was there, in the middle of my bed.'

'So you didn't have to bring it down to the dining room, did you?'

'No, please!' Lady Medd-Hall put her hands together, as if she were praying. 'Jane, my dear, I hardly know what to say . . . this is quite utterly barbaric! It's the dogs, of course; it has to be. They must have found it in the yard. But why they should have felt the need to take it upstairs and visit it upon you, heaven only knows! I can assure you—' she turned, almost tearfully, to Mum and Dad – 'we are *not* rat infested. Just the occasional one – but this is really too much! They'll have to be locked out, if this is the way they're going to behave – Helen, did you hear me? Those dogs will have to be locked out. We cannot have this sort of thing going on.'

'They've never done it before.' Helen stood her ground, defiantly. She had come back into the room followed by Andrew and two eagerly panting dogs.

'Well, they'd better not do it again. Poor Jane has had quite enough to put up with. What must she be thinking of us? You'd better take that quilt away and find another one for her.'

'Did you manage to get it off them?' said Jane, as Helen, with a closed expression on her face, gathered up the quilt.

'At the expense, very nearly, of a finger,' said Andrew.

Lady Medd-Hall tutted, crossly.

'It should have been Helen's finger. They're her animals. She really ought to keep them under better control. I've a good mind—'

'Oh, please,' begged Jane, 'don't blame the dogs.'

She didn't believe the dogs had had anything to do with it. She didn't think that Andrew thought that, either.

'Anyway, it's only fitting it should end up in Jane's room.' That was her dad, trying to lift the tension. 'That'll teach her to go round with a badge saying rats have rights!'

'No, but really,' insisted Lady Medd-Hall, 'it is a great deal too bad. You mustn't think this kind of thing happens *all* the time in the country, Jane. We're normally quite civilized.'

'Which is more than can be said about you,' whispered Jane's mum. 'What a crude and stupid thing to do! Why couldn't you just have come down and taken your dad to one side and told him? He'd have seen to it for you; there wasn't any need to go upsetting everyone like that.'

Never mind me being upset, thought Jane. I suppose I don't count. Moodily, she helped herself to some mashed potatoes.

'There's a letter come for you, by the way. I put it in your room. There wasn't any rat there then,' said Mum. 'I think it's from Lynn,' she added.

It was a postcard, rather than a letter. Lynn must

have dashed it off and posted it the minute she got back home, before Jane's telephone call. Jane read it after lunch, in the privacy of her bedroom (with its new quilt spread over the bed).

> 'Dear Jane, It's you that's changed, not me. I'm just the same I always was. I guess that's the problem. What gets me is that you don't seem to *realize* you've changed; that's the really pathetic thing. I said it would happen, didn't I? Only you didn't believe me. Your once best friend, Lynn.
>
> PS Those clothes are *dire*. You'd have thought so yourself this time a month ago. It just proves my point.'

At least, thought Jane, she had had the decency to put the card in an envelope.

6

Jane woke up the next morning with the whole of her right side aching from the tumble she had taken the day before. It was a struggle to sit up, an agony to climb out of bed. As she perched on the edge, centimetre by painful centimetre pulling on her leggings, she reflected that she had Helen to thank for that. If she hadn't come interfering and laying down the law, Andrew could have taken the horse he wanted and never have found himself galloping off out of control. Helen had obviously known what the horse was like; that was why she had said, 'Don't let it blow itself'. It was obviously in the habit of lighting out.

Jane reached for her top, wincing as she did so. Venomous thoughts filled her head. She wouldn't be at all surprised if Helen had done it on purpose, just to be malicious. It would fit in with her apparent scheme of things: do her best to ensure that Jane had a bad ride and that would be another black mark against coming to live at Shallaford. If she only realized the futility of it! Jane didn't need any convincing, and as for Jane's dad, he was stubborn as a mule. Once he had made his mind up, that was that; nothing that Helen could do, or that Jane could say, would shift him. Jane could have broken her neck and he still wouldn't have budged.

'Much better to have a broken neck in the country than in Shepherd's Bush. Much better for you.'

Helen was simply wasting her time.

Andrew and Helen both appeared at the breakfast table in their riding gear. Andrew pulled an apologetic face at Jane across the table.

'Can't offer you a ride this morning, I'm afraid. I have to take a hack out.'

It was just as well, thought Jane. Not that she was scared; simply that she doubted her ability to climb into the saddle.

'So if you're not going out with your boyfriend,' said Dad, as they left the dining room (Jane winced: did Dad have to?), 'how about coming for a drive? We thought we'd explore some of the countryside, have lunch in a pub, maybe go and have a proper look round Lewes . . . it'd be nice on a Sunday. Nice and quiet. And New Year's Day, as well! We ought to do something.'

'All right,' said Jane. 'I'll come if you like.'

There wasn't anything else to do. She didn't fancy going for a walk by herself, she certainly didn't want to sit and watch television, she was sick of reading her book, so she might just as well go and help pollute the atmosphere a bit more than it already was.

'We could always try walking into Lewes,' she said, but that went down like a lump of black pudding in a goldfish bowl. You didn't walk in the country, you drove; endlessly and aimlessly. *Let's look at this, let's look at that.*

'There's more pollution on the Downs, I bet,' said Jane, 'than there is in the Goldhawk Road.'

'I think not,' said her dad.

'Soon will be,' muttered Jane, 'if we come to live here.'

'That's precisely what I w—' began her dad; but Mum, sitting next to him, must have poked at him or pinched his arm, for he snapped his lips shut and made a great show of pulling out to overtake the car in front. What, Jane wondered, was going on?

After driving mindlessly round half of East Sussex, with Mum exclaiming over village greens and thatched cottages – 'Look, Janey! Isn't that delightful?' – they finally fetched up in Lewes, where Dad parked the car and Jane wobbled out on legs still feeling the after-effects of yesterday's unaccustomed exercise. (Strange how you could be perfectly fit, yet just sitting on a horse for a couple of hours, when you weren't used to it, could practically cripple you.)

'We'll have a little wander,' said Dad, 'then we'll find a pub.'

'There's all sorts of incredibly old buildings here, you know, Jane. Anne of Cleves House . . . we could look at that sometime. I believe there's a museum. And a fifteenth-century bookshop! Imagine that!'

'Oh, there's a lot of history in this place. Some of these narrow streets, for instance . . . twittens, they're called, in the local parlance. Go a long way back, they do.'

'Didn't you say Anglo-Saxon, Neil?'

Dad nodded. 'A feature of Anglo-Saxon defended towns towards the end of the ninth century . . . they used to form boundaries between blocks of properties.' Dad was obviously quoting something he had read in a guidebook. '*Twychene*, the word was, originally.'

Never mind about twychenes, thought Jane; she was starting to feel a bit twitchy herself. What was the purpose of this little jaunt? Why were they trying so hard? Telling her all this historical stuff, in the hope of rousing her interest. (History was one of her subjects: history, economics and English.) It was making her uneasy.

'To think that prehistoric farmers once ploughed here,' panted Dad, rhapsodically, as they toiled up the sheer slope of a cobbled street.

'Prehistoric farmers probably ploughed everywhere,' said Jane.

'Ah, but this place is definitely Anglo-Saxon . . . there's an Iron Age rampart somewhere about.'

Iron Age was too early: the nineteenth century was Jane's period. What were they up to?

She discovered what they were up to as they were sitting over their lunch in a pub specially chosen by Dad from the Good Pub Guide.

'Twelfth century, this is,' said Dad, munching on his ploughman's.

Jane, who had had a ploughman's without the cheese – which virtually only left a pickled onion and a lettuce leaf, but that was the price you paid for sticking to your principles – gazed round, obediently.

'You could do a project on the history of Lewes,' urged her mum.

Jane turned slowly to look at her.

'Why should I want to do a project on the history of Lewes?' What had the history of Lewes to do with Palmerston or Disraeli?

'Well—' Her mum squirmed, uncomfortably. She cast an imploring look at Jane's dad. Dad attempted to spear a pickled onion and missed.

'The fact is—' he attempted it again – 'your mother and I—' the pickled onion shot across the table. Jane fielded it for him – 'have decided, after much discussion—'

'You mustn't think we're going into this lightly, Jane.'

'—after much discussion—' Dad finally gave in and picked up the onion in his fingers – 'to make an offer for Shallaford.'

It was only what she had been expecting, but still her heart plummeted.

'I know you're not happy about it, Janey, love, but it's what we want. We've made up our minds.'

'And we're not changing them,' said Dad.

'Does that mean it's definite?' said Jane, dismally.

'As definite as these things can be.'

'Of course, there's many a slip,' said Mum. 'It'll all be subject to contract.'

'But subject to contract—'

'We'll be starting work on it in the spring.'

'What we thought we'd do, we'd put ours on the market the minute we get back and while things are being sorted out we'll rent somewhere out this way. We've seen a really nice little cottage just outside Lewes.'

'You mean, we're going to move straight away?' Jane was appalled. She had thought it would be months. Didn't these things usually take for ever?

'New start to a new year,' said her mum, brightly.

'Why hang about?' Her dad jutted his jaw.

'Speaking for myself, I can't get out of that hell hole soon enough.'

That hell hole, thought Jane, is where I was brought up – where I've been happy – where all my friends are.

Correction: where all her friends *were*. Lynn was the only one she had ever really been close to.

'Try not to mind too much, lovey.' Her mum reached across, placatingly, to pat her hand. 'We've looked into the schools situation, and if you really don't want to go private—'

'No!' Lynn might accuse her of having changed, but she hadn't changed that much.

'I'm told there's a very good comprehensive in Lewes; the Martello School. It's all girls and it's got an excellent reputation for sending people to university. It's even had people get to Oxford and Cambridge.'

'Oh, wow!' said Jane. 'Oxford and *Cambridge*. I don't want to go to Oxford or Cambridge.'

'No, but I was just telling you.'

'Don't plead with her,' said Dad. 'We've been through enough heartache over this. Why do you think we came down here for a fortnight? Why do you think we didn't put in an offer right away? Pussyfooting round you, that's why!'

'I'm sure you'll like this school just as well as Heathfield, Janey.'

'Possibly,' said Jane. If she and Lynn weren't to be friends any more, she really didn't care where she went. Heathfield *had* been a bit of a dump; it was only Lynn's presence that had made it bearable.

'So will you try to be happy about it? For our sake?'

'Haven't really got much choice,' said Jane, 'have I?' She prodded distastefully at her onion. Nasty slippy things, pickled onions. 'It'll only be for a year or two, anyway. I'll be going to university after that.'

Her mum relaxed.

'I knew you'd be a sensible girl,' she said.

She might be sensible; what about Helen?

'Have you told them yet?'

'We told Lady Medd-Hall this morning.'

Which meant that Lady Medd-Hall would almost certainly have told Helen. A sudden shiver ran through her; big hairy spiders crawling up her spine.

'What's the matter?' said her mum.

'Nothing!' Nothing was the matter. It was ridiculous to be frightened. Helen was only a girl, the same age as herself; there wasn't anything she could actually do. All the same—

'I wish you hadn't said anything till we'd got back home,' muttered Jane.

Andrew invited himself into the guests' sitting room that evening for a game of chess.

'I must warn you that I don't play very well,' he said.

'I must warn you that neither do I,' said Jane.

'So that makes two of us. Are you a good loser?'

'Frightfully sporting.'

'Just as well, because I'm not. I hate to lose anything.'

'What do you do? Throw tantrums?'

'Oh, far worse than that!'

'In that case,' said Jane, 'I'll let you win. Incidentally—' she whispered it across the board as she waited for him to make his opening move –

'about the house . . . you can relax. They're going to put in an offer.'

Andrew's hand hovered over a pawn.

'I know; Aunt Elinor told me.'

'You don't sound exactly overjoyed. I thought you'd be pleased.'

'I am for Aunt Elinor's sake. But someone—' Andrew thrust his pawn into battle – 'isn't going to like it.'

Then someone, thought Jane, would just have to lump it. It was every bit as bad for her as it was for Helen. Just because Shallaford was grand and Shepherd's Bush was grot didn't mean that it wasn't just as much of a wrench to leave it.

'We all have to learn—' Jane snatched up one of her own pawns and shoved it forward – 'to make the best of things.'

Andrew pulled a face. 'Try telling her.'

Mum and Dad went up to bed at ten o'clock, leaving Jane and Andrew still sitting over their chessboard.

'I think we might as well face it,' said Andrew, at last, 'we're neither of us ever going to make grand master . . . want to give up and watch a late-night movie?' He reached across for the *Radio Times*. 'Let's see what we've got . . . how about this? *A mysterious force invests machinery with murderous life* . . . that sounds like a good laugh. Do you fancy it?'

It was the sort of film that would have scared Lynn out of her wits. Andrew and Jane, comfortably snuggled together on the sofa, simply sat and giggled. All the same, Jane was glad she didn't have to go up the stairs by herself afterwards.

'Told you it would be a laugh,' said Andrew. He

flipped the switch on the remote control. 'Haven't seen anything so funny since *Psycho*.'

'*Psycho* was sick,' said Jane.

'But funny.'

'It wasn't funny! Trust a man to think so . . . I bet you wouldn't have thought it so amusing if it had been a guy getting knifed to death.'

'Ugh, no!' Andrew gave a little feminine wriggle accompanied by a small shriek. 'Horrible!'

'You know something?' said Jane. 'I'm almost beginning to be glad that my mum and dad are buying this place . . . it means I'll be going to a school without *any boys at all*. Somewhere civilized, for a change.'

'Go on! You'll hate it. You won't know what to do with yourself.'

'You want to bet?'

'How can I bet,' said Andrew, 'when I haven't a penny to my name?' He suddenly became serious. 'You reckon it's definitely on, then, do you? They're really going to go ahead?'

'Looks like it.'

'I guess Aunt Elinor will have told Helen.'

'I suppose so. Where is she, anyway? I haven't seen her since breakfast.'

'No, it's her day for visiting Toby. I saw her come back but she was in one of her states. Pushed straight past me. She gets very emotional, sometimes, about Toby.'

'I do wish—' Jane hugged her knees, rocking herself on the sofa – 'I do wish I could talk to that girl.' Jane might pride herself on being thick-skinned but she didn't enjoy being on bad terms with people, even with someone as strange and sullen as Helen.

'I don't advise you to try it,' said Andrew.

'But I feel if I could only talk to her – if I could just explain to her that I don't like what's happening any more than she does . . . even if we couldn't be friends, we might at least end up managing to be civil.' And not leaving dead rats on people's beds. 'Honestly,' grumbled Jane, 'it's all so ridiculous.'

Andrew sighed.

'Jane, I'm sorry to say this but – I don't quite know how to put it. Lynn would understand . . . to be perfectly blunt, my cousin Helen is a bit – class-conscious. Your actual dyed-in-the-wool, toffee-nosed aristo.'

The colour rose to Jane's cheeks. She was glad they were sitting in the almost dark.

'You mean she thinks we're beneath her?'

'Not worthy of stepping through the hallowed portals.'

'Why? What does she think we're going to do? Keep coal in the bath? Chop the banisters up for firewood? Have barbecues on the lawn?'

'I think it's more the idea of wet lettuce leaves down the bosom.'

'*Pardon?*' said Jane.

'Oh! You know.' Andrew waved a hand, plainly embarrassed. 'The old picture of the working classes. The *wairkin' clahsses* . . . knocking back the port and lemon and stuffing wet lettuce leaves down mother-in-law's front.'

'Is that what they do?' said Jane.

'Oh, all the time! Their principal occupation. Don't tell me you never have?'

'I've obviously missed out. Give me some wet

lettuce leaves and I'll start practising straight away on Helen. It sounds like a really fun game.'

'Hey, look, don't spit venom at me, lady! It weren't my fault. I was just trying to explain – as nicely as possible – why it is that you won't get any change out of Mistress Helen – even apart from the fact that she hates your guts, and that would apply to anyone who made an offer.'

'Not just us lower-class erks.'

'Anyone,' said Andrew. 'Even the Queen.'

'You think she'd go round leaving dead rats in the middle of the Queen's bed?'

'The dogs might. They know no social distinctions.'

'But it wasn't the dogs, was it?'

Andrew gave it a second before replying.

'We don't know that,' he said.

We do, thought Jane; we just don't want to admit it. Even Andrew, when pushed, would close ranks rather than take the part of an outsider.

'Jane, I'm sorry!' He caught her hands, pulling her up from the sofa. 'I know you think I'm being feeble, but she is my cousin, when all's said and done – and it's not as if we have any actual proof. All the same—' He drew her to him. 'It might be a good idea if you locked your door tonight. Not that I think for one moment she'll try anything, but if she's heard about your parents making an offer she's bound to be feeling a bit disturbed. It might just set her off on her wandering.'

Yes, and she just might come wandering my way, thought Jane.

'If you hear any more voices, or you get scared or anything, you know where my room is? Up the stairs at the end of the passage, last door on the right. You can always come and knock me up – in fact, do come and knock me up. Will you? Promise?'

'It takes a lot to scare me,' said Jane.

'But if anything should—'

'I'll come,' she said.

She had been asleep for what seemed like hours (but turned out to have been only a few minutes) when she was woken by the sound of the underwater voice booming at her down the chimney.

Jane froze where she lay, the covers clutched to her chin, her heart pounding in her rib cage. Despite her bold words earlier, the clammy fingers of fear were already crawling over her skin. Easy enough to be brave and defiant with Andrew holding her close: not so easy all by herself in a locked room.

She forced herself at last to reach out a hand for the bedside lamp. Slowly, still clutching the covers, she edged herself into a sitting position. The voice burbled on, muted waves of menace lapping at her from the hearth.

Well, go on then, big mouth! Do something! thought Jane. Don't just lie here . . . do something!

Snatching at a pillow she sprang from the bed, intending to stuff the pillow up the chimney – anything to drown the obscene babble, but before she could do so, the babble had changed. Had turned to a whisper. Turned to words.

'Look! Look! Out of the window!'

Jane stood, stock still, the pillow in her hands.

'Look! Look!' It came again; cajoling, commanding: hoarse and throaty, from the blackness of

110

the chimney. 'Out of the window! See what's out there . . . out of the window!'

I don't need this, thought Jane. Her lip trembled. What had she ever done to deserve such treatment?

'Look! See! Out of the window!'

Jane took a breath. She could either give in and run to Andrew – or she could look, and refuse to be impressed.

'Helen Medd-Hall—' she said it through gritted teeth – 'you are not going to scare me!'

Tossing the pillow on to the bed, in one swift movement, before she could lose her nerve, Jane darted across to the windows and twitched at a curtain.

The figures were back, bobbing up and down as before over the window ledge; but this time she could see the blood splattered down their cheeks, spurting from their eyes, trickling in gouts from their nostrils . . .

With a shudder of revulsion, she dropped the curtain and ran for Andrew.

'Which window was it?'

'That one.' Jane pointed. 'But it's no good looking, they won't be there now.' The faces would have gone, just as the voice had. And then he would be convinced she was nothing but a hysterical female – or worse still, a conniving one. Anything to lure a man into her bedroom . . .

Briskly, Andrew yanked the curtain back – and of course it was just as Jane had predicted: not a face in sight.

'I knew there wouldn't be! Now you'll think I'm barmy!'

111

Andrew put a finger to his lips. Slowly, making as little noise as possible, he slid the sash window up and leaned out, just as Dad had done.

'They were there!' Jane whispered it urgently. 'I wasn't making it up!'

'I believe you.' Andrew drew back into the room. 'Look at that.'

He held out a finger. Jane recoiled.

'Blood?'

'I'm not sure.' He raised it cautiously to his nostrils. 'Paint!'

'You mean—' Jane faltered. 'They weren't real faces?'

'What did they look like?'

'Horrible!'

'Masks? Could they have been masks?'

'I suppose – they could have been.'

And the paint still wet . . . Jane shivered, as the full implications came home to her. If the paint was wet it meant that Helen must only have just done it. It meant that she had been sitting there, in the middle of the night, in a silent house, daubing faces with red gloss in the vain hope of – what? Scaring Jane out of her senses? Giving her a breakdown? Persuading Mum and Dad, even at the eleventh hour, into changing their minds?

'This is just crazy!' Jane hissed it angrily.

'There are some crazy people around.'

'I th—'

'Sh! We don't want to wake anyone. Have you got a tissue I can use?'

She fetched him one from her bag.

'At least you can't blame this on Lynn!'

'No.' He wiped the paint off his finger, screwed

112

up the tissue and dropped it disdainfully into the wastebasket. 'I can't blame this on Lynn.'

'It can only be her, can't it?' Jane couldn't bring herself to pronounce Helen's name; but Andrew knew whom she meant.

Grimly, he said, 'It's beginning to look that way.'

'But how does she do it? How does she get voices to come down the chimney? How—'

'I don't know,' said Andrew. 'But I shall find out, I promise you.'

7

Gaily, over breakfast, Lady Medd-Hall posed her usual question: 'And what are we all planning to do today?'

It seemed that everyone save Jane was planning to do something. Lady Medd-Hall herself was going up to London to see her solicitor, Andrew was taking her in to Lewes and dropping Helen off on the way. Helen was spending the day with some mad hi-fi cronies at a record fair. Mum and Dad were also going in to Lewes, to put in their offer, and were then driving along the coast to Portsmouth.

'And Jane? What about Jane? Will she be going to Portsmouth?'

'No, I think I'll stay here,' said Jane.

It would give her the opportunity to do some investigating. She had been on a guided tour of the house with Mum and Dad – 'See, Janey, we thought we'd make this bit into a flat for your gran. We thought we might turn this into a sort of games room. Snooker and ping pong, and that. And how about this for your bedroom?' – but she'd never had a chance to look round by herself. The only time she'd penetrated into the family's private quarters had been last night, when she had gone running to wake Andrew. It was not that she had any desire to pry into family secrets, only that there were certain small matters which needed to be cleared up.

I shall find out, I promise you – but could Andrew be trusted to pass on the information to Jane? She was not convinced that he could. He would be too scared that she would spill the beans about his precious cousin. She respected him for his loyalty, but it meant that in the last resort she had no-one but herself to rely on. Mum and Dad were no use: they didn't believe a word that she said.

'Will you be all right?' said Lady Medd-Hall. 'On your own all day?'

'Maybe she needn't be on her own.' Mum beamed round the table with a big mumsy beam. 'Maybe we could take Lady Medd-Hall and Helen into Lewes with us, then Andrew wouldn't have to come.'

Jane cringed. She crimped her hands under the table. Mum, she thought, don't do this to me!

'It's kind of you to offer,' said Andrew, 'but I've got to get the car out, so I might just as well drop off Aunt Elinor and Helen while I'm about it.'

'Well, if you're sure,' said Mum, obviously disappointed.

'Why have you got to get the car out?' That was Helen, coming unexpectedly to life.

Andrew raised an eyebrow.

'Because I've arranged to go and visit friends in Brighton – unfortunately. If I'd known you weren't going to be doing anything, Jane, I'd have put it off to another day. We could have gone for a ride, or something.'

'No, you couldn't,' said Helen. 'Monday is the horses' day off.'

115

'Well, yes, that's why I arranged the visit for a Monday. Obviously.' Helen regarded him darkly, through a thick mane of hair. She seemed to be brooding on something. (Wondering why Jane was still of sound mind and hadn't yet succumbed to the screaming habdabs?) 'But I hardly think a slow walk would have hurt any of them.'

'So are you going to change your mind, Janey, and come with us?'

Jane shook her head.

'No, honestly. I'll be all right.'

'Would you like it, Jane—' Lady Medd-Hall leaned across the table towards her, her bosoms sweeping pieces of toast out of the toast rack – 'if I prepared you a packed lunch, or would you prefer to go and forage for yourself? I'm afraid it's Mrs Fraser's day off, but I'm sure she'll have left something in the freezer . . . When she knew we had a vegan coming she prepared lots of little vegan pies and pasties. They only need popping in the oven.'

'That girl,' said Mum, 'couldn't tell an oven from a spin dryer . . . useless, she is. She can pass her exams all right, no problem about that. But lock her in a kitchen for a few days by herself and she'd starve to death.'

Lady Medd-Hall, whom Jane suspected of having no sense of humour, was looking worriedly at Helen.

'Maybe, Helen, you should stay here and take care of our guest?'

'No!' The word came yelping agitatedly out of Jane's mouth before she could stop it, but was fortunately covered by her dad's forceful, 'Good heavens alive, the girl's quite old enough to take care of herself! If she hasn't learnt to cook by now,

116

that's her problem. Let her starve for a day.'

Andrew caught Jane's eye across the table and winked. Lady Medd-Hall said, 'You come into the kitchen with me, Jane, and we'll see what's what.'

At the last moment, just as everything had been settled – 'That's the oven, Jane. That's the spin dryer.' Maybe she did have a sense of humour, after all – Helen suddenly said, 'I'll stay, if you want.'

Jane stiffened. She saw Andrew frown slightly.

'Really, I'll be perfectly all right,' said Jane. Sooner go to Portsmouth with Mum and Dad than be left in the house with Helen. 'I quite enjoy my own company.'

Helen looked at her a moment, seemed to hesitate, then defiantly slung her hair back over her shoulders and went off to join her mother in the Shallaford Land Rover.

'You're quite sure, Janey—' her mum made one last attempt – 'that you won't come with us?'

'No, truly, Mum. I'll be far happier on my own.'

'All right, then. I'll say bye-bye, love.' Mum planted one of her warm powdery kisses on Jane's cheek. 'We'll see you this evening. Have a good day.'

'And you.'

Andrew, under the pretence – Jane felt sure it was a pretence – of getting out of the Land Rover to check his rear tyres, muttered, 'I'd have cancelled my trip if Helen had stayed. Are you sure you'll be OK?'

'Of course I will,' said Jane. She just wanted them to be on their way now, so that she could get down to business.

'We should be back round about four-thirty. I'm picking Helen and Aunt Elinor up at the station at

117

four. Oh, and Jane . . . I haven't forgotten what I promised.'

Jane watched as the Land Rover, followed by Mum and Dad's car, disappeared down the drive. She went back indoors, waited a few minutes to make sure they were all safely gone, then set off on her tour of the house. The two dogs accompanied her, padding watchfully at her heels, tails wagging and noses to the ground – whether to keep an eye on her or out of simple curiosity, she could not be sure.

The doors marked 'Private' on the ground floor had both been left unlocked. It was an open invitation – and yet she hesitated to go in. It reeked too much of snooping, for she could hardly imagine Helen would have left any traces of her handiwork lying about in her mother's own sitting rooms.

She remained for several seconds, her hand on the doorhandle, before finally overcoming her scruples.

It was a different world in the family's private quarters. Thick rugs lay scattered over polished wood-block floors. The furniture was almost certainly antique (though she could see where the cats had been allowed to dig their claws in). Paintings in thick gilt frames adorned the walls – real paintings; not the Boots reproductions that Jane's mum had always had to make do with. A grand piano stood open in one corner.

Jane wandered as if in an Aladdin's cave, threading her way amongst the various pieces of furniture. On a side table stood a photograph, a portrait of a young boy, perhaps twelve or thirteen years old. It had to be Toby, for it bore a striking resemblance to Helen – the same dark, deep-set eyes and prominent aquiline nose, the same thick black hair growing from a peak low on the forehead.

Jane stood for a long while, considering it, trying to trace signs of the illness which had ultimately overcome him. She couldn't: he looked like any other young boy. Certainly nowhere near as intense as his sister, whose portrait stood by his side on the same table. Helen, even at twelve or thirteen, had had the hooded eyes, the guarded expression that she wore now. You could tell, thought Jane, that Helen was going to grow up to be troubled; not Toby.

She left the room, carefully shepherding the dogs before her and closing the door behind them. Where next?

Stairs at the back of the house leading down to a basement area initially seemed promising but, upon inspection, the basement turned out to be merely a repository for what she could only describe as family junk. She prowled amongst it for a while but it was dark down there, and cold, lit only by small yellow bulbs hanging naked from the ceiling, and no form of heating that she could discover. The dogs showed no interest, declining to come with her, though one of the cats slunk in and refused to come out so that she was forced to leave it there, with the door slightly ajar, and hope that it emerged before the family returned. She wouldn't like it thought that she had been poking into other people's possessions. She *was* doing so, of course; but not out of nosiness.

The dogs were waiting for her, side by side, in the hall.

'Let's go upstairs,' said Jane.

They heaved themselves enthusiastically to their feet and lolloped up the stairs ahead of her. She was glad of their company in the empty house. She had never minded being on her own in Shepherd's Bush, in spite (as her dad never ceased to remind her) of the far higher incidence of crime in built-up areas; but the house in Shepherd's Bush was small and compact, not to say positively cramped. In the depths of winter you could bolt the front door and feel yourself enclosed in a nest.

There was nothing nest-like about Shallaford. In summer, perhaps, with shafts of sunlight to brighten it, it might be more friendly, less barren; but on a grey winter's morning, with little natural light to illuminate the dark corners, the place was full of shadows, all potentially threatening.

Jane set off along the upstairs corridor. Every door she opened gave on to a perfectly ordinary bedroom. The only one that was locked was the cupboard next to the room in which Mum and Dad slept. She remembered that she had once met Helen coming from the direction of the cupboard; could that be where she hatched her secrets? There was no way of finding out for she hadn't a key and didn't know where one might be. In the kitchen, perhaps? On a hook? Or did Helen carry it round with her? It seemed significant, the more she thought about it, that the door should be locked. You would imagine that an upstairs cupboard might contain bed linen, and who would want to lock up bed linen? Guests weren't very likely to make off with the sheets and pillowcases. She determined that she would look in the kitchen when she went back down.

In the meanwhile, there was the upper floor to be explored. She made her way boldly up the stairs, past the bathroom, trying not to feel guilty, like a Peeping Tom. The dogs preceded her, tails held high. The room they stopped at had to be Helen's. She knew, from hearing Lady Medd-Hall inveigh against it at the breakfast table – 'Those wretched dogs, Helen, with their filthy paws!' – that they slept at night on Helen's bed. She reached out for the handle, and as she did so the telephone shrilled from the floor below.

The sudden sound in the empty house made her jump. She thought at first that she wouldn't answer it, but then she thought, 'It could be Andrew.' Andrew, saying he had cancelled his visit after all and was coming back to keep her company. Jane turned, and went bounding down the stairs.

Breathlessly, she snatched up the receiver.

'Hello?'

A voice at the other end – high and fluting: she couldn't tell whether it was a child's or an old woman's – said, 'Who am I speaking to? Is that Jane?'

'Yes,' said Jane. Already, she didn't know why – except how many people knew that she was there? – her skin was starting to prickle. 'Who is that?'

From the other end of the telephone came a thin, reedy chuckle.

'Never mind who it is, my dear. I have a message for you . . . are you sitting comfortably? Are you listening? You're going to die, Jane. Jane's going to die.'

Jane felt the pit of her stomach grow cold with fear.

'Helen?' she whispered. 'Is that you?'

Again, the thin reedy chuckle.

'Wouldn't you like to know?'

Jane tightened her grip on the telephone.

'Why are you doing this to me? I don't want to come and live in your house! It's not my fault!'

'You're still going to die, Jane. I've made up my mind . . . Jane's going to die. I'm going to kill you, Jane.'

'Well, screw you!' shouted Jane.

She banged down the receiver. With her heart thudding in her rib cage, she half ran, half fell, down the stairs, snatched her anorak from where she had left it on the newel post, and went racing out of the house. The dogs, barking clamorously, raced with her.

'Go back! You two, go back!'

Ignoring their protests, she thrust them hysterically through the front door, slamming it shut behind her. Only then did she think to feel in her pockets. She had the front-door key – Lady Medd-Hall had given it her this morning, for what it was worth, which was precisely nothing since wild horses wouldn't drag her back into the house by herself. The very thought made her flesh start to crawl – but the only money she had on her was a handful of loose change. That wasn't going to take her very far. What was she to do now?

Jane zipped up her anorak. She would walk. She would walk to the nearest village and she would go to the police. She would tell the police everything and if the story got into the local papers and shamed them that was just too bad. Mum and Dad refused to believe anything she told them, and Andrew, for all his promises, chose to go cavorting off to visit friends rather than stay behind and help her investigate. Why should she worry about his tender feelings?

She struck off along the lane which led to the main road. She had covered only about a hundred metres when the Shallaford Land Rover came lurching round the corner. It pulled to a halt beside her, and Andrew jumped out.

'Jane! Where are you off to?'

Before she could stop herself, she had burst into tears. (She *loathed* women who behaved like that.)

'I'm g-going to the p-police!'

'What? Why? What's happened? Janey—' He took her into his arms, holding her tight against him. 'You're frightened! Something's happened to frighten you!'

Sobbing, she told him the story of the telephone call.

'I'm sick of it! It's been going on ever since I got here! It's making my life a misery!'

'And you feel that no-one's doing anything about it. And you're quite right.' Andrew said it sombrely. 'No-one is – including me. That's why I came back. I suddenly felt incredibly guilty, going off to have a good time and leaving you here on your own. Also, I've been having thoughts . . . Jane, listen!' He tilted her chin towards him with the tip of a finger. 'If you really want to go to the police, I'll take you. I'll drive you into Lewes straight away. But I think I may have cracked what's been going on – and how she's been doing it.'

'Helen?'

'Well—' He hesitated. 'I guess it's not very likely to be Aunt Elinor.'

'But at least you admit that it's someone!'

'I've never really doubted that it was someone. I suppose, if I'm to be honest, I've never really doubted that it was Helen.'

'Even that first telephone call?'

'Even that first telephone call. I'm sorry, Janey! I shouldn't have tried to put the blame on Lynn. But it's not easy – when it's your own cousin—'

'Look, I don't want to get her into trouble,' cried Jane, 'I just want her to stop it!'

'There won't be any trouble, but she needs some kind of help. It's been glaringly obvious for ages, only I've been too much of a coward to say anything to Aunt Elinor, and Aunt Elinor's been too busy trying to make a go of Shallaford and come to terms with – with Toby's illness. It was up to me, and that's why I feel guilty. If I'd had the courage to face facts months ago, long before you ever came here, none of this would ever have happened. So, it's up to you, Janey . . . you can jump in the wagon and I'll take you in to Lewes, or you can give me this one last chance to redeem myself.'

'It's all right.' Jane blotted at her eyes with a scrap of screwed-up tissue. 'I didn't really want to go to the police, it was just that I didn't know what else to do. I couldn't face the thought of spending the rest of the day shut up in that house all by myself!'

'Well, you're not by yourself now, you've got me. So, are you game?'

'If we're really going to do something,' said Jane.

'We are really going to do something. I told you, I've been having thoughts . . . here! Hop in.'

Jane climbed into one side of the Land Rover, Andrew the other. In less than a minute, they were scrunching back over the gravel, up the drive to Shallaford.

'Before we go in—' Andrew parked round the side and held out his hand for Jane's – 'come and have a look at the back of the house. I want to show you something.' He led her round there, her hand in his. 'Look! You see that parapet?'

Jane looked, and nodded.

'There's a flat roof behind that – well, more a sort of walkway. Now, your bedroom is . . . which one? That second one along; directly beneath the parapet. Right?'

She nodded again. 'Mm.'

'And your chimney is . . . one of that cluster there. I don't know which one, but I imagine it would be pretty simple to find out.'

'You mean, she – she could have got on the flat roof—'

'And put whatever she liked down your chimney. Precisely.'

'How would she have got up there?'

'Easy; there's a door that leads on to it from the other end of the passage on our floor.'

'But—' Jane frowned, as she tried to picture it. 'How would she have managed the faces?'

He hunched a shoulder.

'Attached them to something? Dangled them off the roof?'

'Down to my bedroom.'

'And then hoicked them up again when she reckoned you'd had enough.'

'But what about last night? They were there when I came to get you—'

'And gone by the time I arrived. I know; I've been

thinking about that. Either she was still hiding out on the roof, or—' his eyes travelled further along the parapet – 'or she scuttled off back to her den.'

Jane's eyes, following his gaze, came to rest on the circular turret at the corner of the house.

'You mean, you can get in there?'

'There's an entrance from the flat roof, and another down below, at the end of your corridor. Do you want me to make a confession? Do you want me to tell you why I really felt so guilty? It's because it suddenly struck me, over breakfast . . . that could be where she's operating from. But because I'm a selfish swine I thought I'd leave it till I got back. And then I realized you were going to be here on your own, so I – I swiped the key on my way out. Just as a precaution. It's been burning a hole in my pocket all the way to Lewes. In the end I just had to turn back – and thank God I did! Do you feel strong enough to come exploring, or—'

'Yes!' She was eager to make amends for her earlier display of weakness. 'Are you talking about that door next to Mum and Dad's room? I wondered why it was locked.'

'It isn't, as a rule. Nobody ever goes there except Helen – it's her hideaway. Where she crawls like a wounded animal when things have got too much for her. I'm not absolutely certain what we're going to find there, if anything, but we might as well take a look.'

As they opened the front door, the dogs greeted them, boisterously. Andrew kicked at them.

'Down, you!'

'Oh, don't!' begged Jane. 'They're confused . . . they thought I was going to take them for a walk.'

126

'They're nothing but a nuisance. Helen lets them do whatever they want. Go on!' He thrust open one of the doors marked 'Private'. 'Get in there and shut up! OK?' He turned to Jane. 'You ready? Still game?'

'Lead on,' said Jane.

It was amazing how the simple fact of having Andrew at her side made the house immediately less threatening; in fact, not really threatening at all. It put everything into a different perspective. So some pathetic unbalanced girl made vindictive telephone calls and played a few stupid tricks; so what? It was nothing Jane couldn't cope with. She was mainly interested in discovering how it had all been done – and making sure that it didn't go on being done.

'We'll go up this way.' Andrew pointed along the corridor towards the bathroom end.

'Not through the cupboard?' said Jane, disappointed.

'What cupboard?'

She gestured to the door next to her parents' room. 'The one you've got the key of.'

'We'll come back that way. It's not actually a cupboard; it's just steps leading up to the turret room. But I want to try the other exit to see if it opens easily. In theory it shouldn't, because in theory no-one ever goes out there. So if it does—'

'It means she's been going in and out that way.'

'It means someone has.'

Even now he was trying to keep up the pretence that it might not be Helen. But who else could it be? Who else was there?

They walked up the stairs to the Medd-Halls' private corridor, where scarcely half an hour since, Jane had been prowling on her own.

'That's Helen's bedroom,' said Andrew. 'That's Aunt Elinor's. That of course is mine. That one—' he paused. 'That one used to be Toby's. They still keep it ready for him. Just in case he should ever come back.'

'Will he?' said Jane.

'No.' Andrew said it shortly. 'Never.'

They went up another flight of stairs, cramped and steep, to a small door at the top which gave on to the roof. Andrew reached for the upper bolt: it slid open, soundlessly. He looked at Jane and pulled a face, then stooped to try the bottom one. That also slid open. Jane felt her stomach begin to churn – with excitement rather than fear.

'Right,' said Andrew. 'Here we go.'

They stepped out on to a narrow walkway, which seemed for some reason immediately familiar. Instinctively, Jane hesitated. Andrew looked at her, concerned.

'You're not scared of heights?'

She wasn't, normally. Why today? And then she turned her head and saw the roof rising steeply behind her, and she knew why: she had been here before, in her dream. She had walked on a narrow path, high up, with what she had thought was a slag heap towering behind her and a sheer drop on the other side. She shivered slightly.

'Would you rather go back in?' said Andrew.

'No.' Jane forced herself to stand, holding on to the edge of the parapet and gazing out at the Downs, rolling into the far distance, and the Shallaford gardens below.

'Quite a drop, isn't it?' Andrew joined her, leaning over to look down. 'But we're not here to admire

the view. To business! Your window must be about
. . . about here? Would you say? Yes! Take a look
at this.' Jane shuffled along to where he was pointing. 'X marks the spot! How about that for a piece
of detection work?'

Someone had placed two yellow chalk marks,
about fifteen centimetres apart, on the top of the
parapet.

'Let's go and have a look in the turret room.'

The door into the turret room opened on to a small
circular space with bare stone walls and the floor
covered in a scattering of rugs. Two slit windows
let in a rather dim light. A windowseat, roughly
constructed, had been built beneath them. The only
other furniture was an old folding table covered in
tattered green baize. On the table stood a cardboard
box – and a tape recorder. Andrew dived at once
into the box.

'Masks!' He swung them into the air. 'Are these
what you saw?'

They dangled before her, bobbing up and down
as they had outside her window. Their faces were
streaked with red paint.

'Yes.' She stared at them, repelled yet fascinated.
'Yes! That's exactly what I saw.'

'Ingenious.' Andrew dropped them back into the
box. 'They say the simplest ideas are always
the best.'

'What about this?' Jane had turned her attention
to the tape machine. There was no electric point
in the turret room, but a length of flex had been
crudely run up from the floor below. (She remembered the day of the heavy breathing, with her
and Helen alone in the house, and Helen crouched

in the hall, doing things with wires.) 'How does it play?'

Andrew leaned across and pressed a switch. Immediately, the sound of the underwater voice filled the room.

'That's it!' said Jane. 'That's what it was!'

'That's at half-speed,' said Andrew. 'If we play it at full speed—'

He leaned across again, and turned the switch another notch. Now the voice wasn't underwater any more. Now Jane could hear what it was saying.

'Look! Look! Out of the window!'

She could also hear who was saying it.

8

'You!'

Already the fear fingers were creeping. Instinctively she backed away from him, towards the door, but he was there before her.

'Yes!' He gave her his funny lopsided smile; sinister now, rather than attractive. 'Me, all along . . . and you never guessed it, did you? You hadn't the least idea. *Helen!*' He imitated Jane's voice on the telephone. *'Why are you doing this to me? I don't want to come and live in your house! It's not my fault!'* And there I was, only five minutes away, speaking on my little carphone . . . and that other time! What was it you said? *Lynn, if that's you, you're a moron!'*

He laughed; and soft though it was, it was a spine-chilling sound.

'Poor old Helen, getting all the blame! I really fooled you there, didn't I? You really thought it was her. Confess it! You did, didn't you?'

Terrified, Jane nodded.

'Or did you think it was Toby? Poor, mad Toby . . . did it ever cross your mind that it might be him, escaped from the loony bin? No? He was my back-up; my second suspect.' Andrew giggled.

'I was the very last person . . . 'cause I've been so

nice to you, haven't I? Haven't I, Janey? I've been so nice and Helen's been so nasty.'

He giggled again; a small contented sound rather like a cat purring. 'She's a snooty cow, I grant you, but totally spineless. You really think she'd have been capable of wringing old Charlie's neck and stuffing him down the chimney? I bet she cried her eyes out when she discovered it was him! You'd get on well with Helen – if ever you were likely to have the opportunity. Which now, of course, you're not.'

He took a step towards her. Jane fled, precipitately, behind the table.

'Oh, it's all right, you've a while to go yet.' He looked at his watch. 'There's no hurry. No-one's going to disturb us. If the condemned man is allowed to eat a hearty breakfast, I don't see why the condemned woman shouldn't be allowed a few last words; do you?'

Jane swallowed. She remembered how Mum had kissed her goodbye, her face all warm and powdery. She remembered the smell of her scent – *La Tropicana*; her favourite. She remembered how she had got into the car and wound down the window to wave, and how they had driven off, happy and unsuspecting, never doubting that Jane would be there waiting for them when they arrived back. It was so unfair! So unfair to Mum and Dad! They had worked hard all their lives and now, when they were looking forward to being able to enjoy themselves, this appalling thing was going to come upon them. The tears started to her eyes.

'Oh, please!' begged Andrew. 'Don't let's have any of that! We've done that scene once. What's happened to your fighting spirit? I loved it when I was talking to you on the telephone . . . *Jane, you're going to die!*' He spoke in the same thin, reedy tones that Jane had been unable to identify. '*You're going to die, Jane* . . . and you thought it was Helen . . . *Well, screw you!* I really liked that. I thought we might have some fun. I never thought you'd turn into a watering-can.'

Jane scrubbed at her eyes; not to please him but because, even now, she despised weakness.

'That's better,' said Andrew. 'That's more like! I can't stand sacrificial victims . . . lambs to the slaughter. It turns my guts. But of course you wouldn't know anything about that, would you? Being—' he curled his lip – 'a *vegan*.'

She found her voice. 'What's wrong with being a vegan?'

'Ah! She speaks! In her south suburban whinge . . . *Jyney.*'

Jane drew herself up. 'That's not south suburban, that's London.'

'*Aow? Lunnun?* I do beg your *pawdon*.'

She looked at him, coldly. 'Why are you doing this to me?' she said.

'What? Planning to kill you?'

The chill fingers of fear went pattering up her spine.

'Any of it! The whole thing! The faces, the voices—'

'Did you like the voices? I practised them for hours in my bedroom. I used to think I might quite like to be an actor – I'm rather good at acting. *To be or not to be—*' he flung out his arms – '*that is the question.* And the answer, unfortunately, in your case, is yes.'

He smiled once again his crooked smile. 'To be! To be! It has to be.'

Jane suppressed a shiver. 'I asked you a question.'

'Did you? Yes! What was it?'

'Why have you done all this?'

'Why have I done all this? You mean, why have I persecuted you? But I've already told you! I've spent hours explaining to you . . . because I don't want Shallaford—' his voice rose, sharply, to a shriek – 'falling into the hands of jumped-up little nobodies who don't even know which knife and fork to use! And then when you do use them you're like a grotesque family of Neanderthals . . . sitting with them stuck up in the air and your mouths wide open!' He mimicked Jane's family, eating. 'You've got no breeding, you've got no culture, you're nothing but clods! That *dad* of yours slumped like some great mindless lump in his cardigan before the telly, and your *mum* reeking of that cheap muck she sprays all over herself . . . it makes me sick just to be in the same room with her! And then your voices . . . *That gel couldn' tella nuven from a spin droyer. Yewless, she is.*'

Jane flushed. 'So you're the snob,' she said, 'not Helen.'

'Snob? What kind of a word is snob? What is *snob* supposed to mean? I don't have such a word in my vocabulary. But if you mean do I object to a family of nouveau riche oiks coming and vandalizing Shallaford then yes, all right, I plead guilty. I've dreamed of living in this house all my life – and a lousy rotten life it's been, too! You don't know what it's like to have your parents break up and not be wanted by either one of them, shunted back and forth, can't be got rid of quickly enough – *Here, you have him, I've done my stint!* I used to come here and I used to resent those two, Master Toby and Mistress Helen . . . had everything on a plate and just took it all for granted. Well, I didn't take it for granted, and I'll fight tooth and nail to hang on to it!'

'But what is the point?' Jane had this desperate feeling that at all costs she must keep him talking. 'What is the point when you said yourself there isn't enough money to look after it properly?'

'I'd find the money! Money isn't important. It's the house that's important.'

'But it would fall into ruins,' pleaded Jane. 'Surely it's better to let someone like Dad have it and—'

'*No!*' He howled it at her. His face twisted. Hatred raged in his eyes. Jane cringed behind the table. (Why, oh why, hadn't she gone to judo classes when Lynn had wanted her to?) 'No!' With an effort, he brought himself back under control. 'Someone like your dad is not going to have it. No-one is going to have it. I'm going to have it. Helen and that ridiculous mother of hers can do what they like. Tell me, Janey!' His voice suddenly changed, became soft and almost honeyed. 'Were you frightened by the things I did? What frightened you most?'

'N-nothing.' Jane said it staunchly. 'Nothing actually frightened me. I just thought it rather ch-childish and s-silly.'

His face darkened. 'Liar! If you weren't frightened, why were you running away?'

'I told you, because I'd had enough of it! I was going to go to the police.'

'And what do you think they'd have done? Locked you up for being batty, I expect.'

'I'm not the one that's batty!' The words had slipped out before she could stop them.

'Are you accusing me?' He closed in on her, leaning across the table, hissing into her face. She could see a vein throbbing in his temple, and the curious yellow glow in his eyes. 'Are you saying' – his voice dropped to a menacing whisper – 'that I'm mad?'

'No!' Jane cast round, panic-stricken, for something with which to defend herself. There was nothing. 'Of course I'm not saying you're mad.'

'Yes, you are! You think I'm round the twist. Don't you? You think I'm certifiable! Just because I'm prepared to kill for something I believe in. You can't understand that, of course. Your sort don't. You're just scum!'

He spat it at her; literally. A blob of spittle landed on her cheek, but she didn't dare lift a hand to wipe it off.

He turned away, in contempt – and spun back again, quick as a flash, as Jane made a movement.

'Stay where you are! I like you there. I've gone to a lot of trouble over you . . . *Janey*. These masks, for instance—' He danced them up and down before her. She saw they were on long lengths of almost invisible nylon cord. 'I had to drive all the way in to Brighton for them. Couldn't afford to buy them locally; someone might have recognized me. I got them in a theatrical shop. Nice, aren't they? I picked the ugliest ones I could find, naturally. Did you notice how ugly they were? How much were you able to see, when you looked out of the window?'

'N-not very much,' said Jane.

'You mean, I could have picked just any old

136

masks?' He sounded disappointed. 'I went to great pains to find these . . . still, never mind! You can see them now. Do you like the blood? I splashed that on at the last moment – I was in two minds whether to bother or not. But then, I thought, you weren't as impressed by the rat as you should have been. That was an act of defiance, Janey, wasn't it? Bringing it downstairs like that. Mind you, it quite amused me. But you had to be punished; I couldn't let you get away with it. You thought it was real blood, didn't you? When I showed it to you on my finger . . . Ugh! Blood! Horrible! I really had you fooled there for a minute, didn't I?'

Jane nodded, weakly.

'I could have had you that night, if I'd wanted. You'd have let me do anything I liked. Wouldn't you? I thought about it . . .' He swung the masks, carelessly. 'I could have given you a thrill. 'Cause you're probably still a virgin, aren't you, Janey? Still a nice little untouched virgin.'

She couldn't decide whether it would be wiser to say yes or to say no, but he carried on without waiting for an answer.

'Don't get your hopes up. I wouldn't touch you with a barge pole! It's what that great shapeless lump you call your mother's been angling for, isn't it? *Maybe Jane needn't be alone . . . maybe Andrew could stay with her.* Maybe they might get all lovey-dovey and a beautiful romance might blossom. *You must be joking!* Andrew doesn't consort with *plebs*. Couldn't even sit on a horse without falling off. And then they think they're going to come here and take over Shallaford. *YOU ARE OUT OF YOUR MIND!'*

The words went screaming round the turret room, bouncing off the bare stone walls.

'*YOU ARE INSANE!*'

'I don't want to take over Shallaford!' cried Jane. 'Why blame me?'

'Because you belong to them! Because you're one of them! You come here, like a parcel of day-trippers with your kiss-me-quick hats and your candyfloss and your ugly whining voices—'

From the bottom of the house, the dogs started barking.

Andrew glanced again at his watch.

'Time, I think. I'm enjoying this conversation, but it can't go on all day. The sooner we get the business over with, the better. Don't you think?' He turned to her, pleasantly. 'You wouldn't want to be kept hanging around all day, would you?'

'What—' the inside of her mouth had gone dry; her tongue felt like a strip of old leather. 'What are you – going to do – with me?'

'Janey, Janey, I thought I'd made that quite clear? I'm going to kill you, Janey.'

'But if you kill me,' she wailed, 'what difference will it make? Mum and Dad will still buy the house!'

'I don't think so, Janey; not when they arrive back to find what a nasty horrid accident their little girl has had. They would need to be somewhat insensitive. And they're not insensitive, are they? Well, the big lumping telly addict might be, but the shapeless mass isn't, is she? She loves her Janey, doesn't she? *I'll say bye-bye, lovey*—' He blew a kiss at her, across the table. 'Bye-bye, Janey! Say bye-bye, Janey!'

Jane shrank back, against the wall. Her eyes slid

sideways to the steps leading down to the next floor. He noticed, and laughed.

'No exit that way, Janey! Andy has the key . . . remember?' He took it from his pocket and swung it tantalizingly, just out of reach. 'You can't get out without the key, and you can't get the key away from Andy. It would be silly to try, wouldn't it? 'Cause if you did, Andy might have to hurt you.'

He was going to hurt her anyway, but she knew she didn't stand a chance of wresting the key from him. Slim though he was, he was certainly a great deal stronger than she was.

'Come along, Janey!' He held out a hand. 'Time to go.'

She stood her ground. 'Go where?'

'Over the top.' He seemed surprised that she should feel the need to ask the question. 'Where else?'

'Look, this is ridiculous! Everyone will know it's you! They'll lock you away, th—'

'Oh, no, Janey! I don't think so. How can I be held responsible? I'm not here, am I? I'm in Brighton. Did you notice, incidentally, the cunning way I parked out of sight, round the side of the house?' He tapped a finger to his forehead. 'I think you'll agree, I've got what it takes. I shall tell them, when we all get back and discover your poor smashed body, how you came running to me last night with some gibberish about seeing faces at the window. I shall tell them how you wanted to get up on the flat roof and explore, and I wouldn't let you. They will naturally conclude – what else can they conclude, Janey? – that you found your way up there while everyone was out and took a tumble over the top. What could be neater? It's all fallen in very nicely.'

'What would you have done—' she squirmed away from him, round the table – 'if I'd said I was going to Portsmouth with Mum and Dad?'

'I would have bided my time. There would have been other opportunities.'

'I suppose that's what you were trying to do the other day.' She edged, slowly, towards the door which led on to the roof. 'When you took me out on that ride.'

'No, no, no! That would have been crude.'

'And you think this isn't?'

'I lost control.' His hands clenched. 'It was your fault, you stupid bitch!'

'How was it my fault?' said Jane, positioning herself for a headlong dash. 'What did I do?'

'*It's only Victorian, isn't it?*' He put on the whining drone that was his Jane voice. '*I know it's a nice house and all that, but it's not anything special.* Well, it's special to me! Do you hear me?' He made a lunge at her, cutting her off from her one escape route. 'It's special to me!'

'So why put it in jeopardy? Why run the risk of never seeing it again?'

He stopped. 'What do you mean, never seeing it again?'

'Well, if they shut you away—'

'I've told you, they won't shut me away!'

'They will if they discover it was you, and they will discover it was you! They're bound to find out you were here. They'll check your alibi – they'll ask your friends in Brighton!'

'I haven't got any friends in Brighton.'

'Then you won't have any alibi! And they'll find the tyre marks, they'll find your fingerprints—'

'Of course they will! Why shouldn't they? I live here. And what's more, I'm going to go on living here. You're procrastinating, Janey. Just trying to put off the evil moment.'

'Well, wouldn't you?' she cried. 'Look, if you want the house as badly as all that, I'll tell Dad. I'll tell him not to buy it, I'll tell him you're—'

'What?' said Andrew. 'What will you tell him? Tell him I'm insane? Tell him I threatened you? Why should he believe that any more than he believed the faces at the window? He knows you're just a little liar, Janey. Just a fantasist. Come!'

He made another lunge. Jane ducked under his outstretched arm and fled in her panic towards the steps leading down to the next floor.

'I told you, Janey—' he leapt after her, grabbing her by the hair and pulling her to him – 'the door is locked: I have the key. Stop wasting my time!'

From somewhere down below, the dogs barked again. They sounded much nearer than they had before; almost as if they were at the foot of the steps, on the other side of the door.

'Who let those bloody dogs out?' screamed Andrew.

'I did.'

Andrew spun round, his grip on Jane's hair relaxing just sufficiently for her to drag herself free and dive for cover. Helen stood framed in the entrance, a shotgun in her hands: it was pointed at Andrew.

'Just because I refuse to go out slaughtering

wildlife,' said Helen, 'don't be fooled into thinking that I don't know how to use this thing – or that I won't use it, if you push me. I assure you, I'm quite capable . . .'

9

The weather was cold for the middle of March. A chill wind blew from the Downs, sweeping across the Martello School playing-field. Jane walked with her head down, her hands dug deep into the pockets of her anorak. Helen, in the pale blue duffel coat which had been the uniform of her previous school, walked at her side.

'I'm really glad,' said Jane, 'that we can talk at last.'

Three months had passed; three months in which the Lawlors had put their house up for sale, packed what few of their possessions they wanted to keep and decamped to their rented cottage on the outskirts of Lewes.

'Are you sure you don't mind, Janey?' At the last moment, Mum had been anxious. 'After everything you've been through . . . we can always withdraw the offer, if you'd rather. It's not as if Shallaford's the only property on the market.'

But Shallaford was what they had set their hearts on, and Jane couldn't bring herself to deny it to them.

Now she and Helen walked round the playing-field, in a state almost of companionship.

'There's something I've been wanting to ask you

for ages,' said Jane. 'You know that day—' That dreadful day – 'when you suddenly appeared holding that shotgun, or whatever it was—'

A perceptible tremor ran through Helen.

'I know. I don't like to think of it, either,' said Jane, 'but somehow I just can't seem to help it. I keep going back to it, over and over.'

'Especially at night,' said Helen.

'Yes.' Jane nodded. 'You wake up and start replaying it. It nearly drives you mad.'

'I have to sing bits of music to myself. It's the only thing that gets rid of it.'

'I recite poetry,' said Jane. 'Only then that starts going round and round as well.'

'At least it's better than the other.'

Anything was better than the other. The other was like a nightmare.

'What I wanted to ask you, though,' said Jane, 'was did you really know how to use it? That gun? Would you have known what to do if he'd – if he'd rushed you?'

'Hadn't a clue,' said Helen. 'It was one of the ones Dad and Toby used to use for shooting game. I never went with them. I hate shooting! I hate hunting, too, in spite of what Andrew may have told you.'

'Andrew told me lots of things.' Jane said it sombrely. She was beginning to wonder just how much of it she could believe.

'What did he tell you? Tell me some of the things that he told you!'

'He told me – that your brother—'

'Toby? What did he tell you about Toby?'

'He told me that he was—'

'What?'

144

'In an institution.'

'Did he tell you why he was in an institution?'

'He made it sound as if he were . . . unstable.'

In tones carefully devoid of emotion, Helen said, 'He's in what they call a persistent vegetative coma. He's been like it for over a year. Mum still believes that one day he'll come out of it, even though the doctors have told her there isn't a chance. But you can't stop people from hoping.'

Jane stared at Helen, appalled. 'How did it—'

'He crashed his car. They said he must have been going too fast. We all believed it because – well! Because he'd only just passed his test and the car was quite a powerful one. And anyhow, it's the way young men behave, isn't it?' Helen said it bitterly. 'Even I was prepared to believe it.'

'You mean you don't now?'

'I've been doing a lot of thinking just recently. I can't help remembering . . . the day that it happened. They were going off together to look at some horses; him and Andrew. They'd got it all arranged. Then at the last moment Andrew decided against it. *Literally* at the last moment. I remember he got into the car and then got out again. He said he felt sick. And I remember thinking that Toby would be glad, because he and Andrew really didn't get on. It was Andrew who'd insisted on going with him. He was the one who'd suggested it. And then when he heard about the accident he kept saying it was all his fault and if only he'd been there it would never have happened, and if he had been there I don't think it *would* have happened because—'

'You think he did something to the car?'

'You see—' Helen picked a strand of hair off her

face – 'I remember him being out there, that morning, before breakfast. I remember because the dogs were out there with him, and I went to see where they were, and he was there, messing about under the bonnet. I didn't think anything about it at the time, it's just now – after all that's happened – I can't help wondering.'

'But if he'd done something,' said Jane, 'wouldn't they have been able to check?'

'Not necessarily; the car was a total wreck. There are things you can do,' said Helen, 'if you know your way round cars. Which Andrew does.'

Jane suddenly shivered.

'I'm sorry!' Helen stretched out a hand, impulsively: the first time she had ever made such a gesture. 'I'm upsetting you.'

'No, it's all right.' Jane shook her head. 'I was just remembering what he said to me, that day in the turret room . . . *I'm prepared to kill for something I believe in.*'

'He tried to kill Toby; I'm sure he did. Even now, when Toby's finally allowed to die, it'll be Andrew who inherits the title. He'd have inherited the house, too, if – if things had worked out differently. If he could have persuaded Mum not to sell it.'

'And my mum and dad not to buy it.'

Helen's mouth twitched. 'He certainly did his best.'

They walked on, past a group of girls from their year. Someone spoke to them, but they were too preoccupied to notice.

'He tried to make me believe it was you doing all those things, you know.' Jane said it remorsefully. She had actually swallowed every single thing that

146

Andrew had said to her. 'He kept telling me you were unbalanced.'

Helen gave a little laugh; not quite steady.

'I couldn't very well blame you if you believed him. I know I'm – not very good at – communicating with people. Only if it's someone like your dad.'

'Because you share the same interest.'

'Yes.' Helen suddenly came alive. There was real enthusiasm in her voice. 'I'm going to come round and listen to his system when you've moved in and he's got it properly set up.'

Jane groaned. 'Dad and his system!'

'No, I'm looking forward to it,' said Helen.

'Doesn't it bother you, the way he speaks?' Jane couldn't resist the jibe. 'That terrible accent of his?'

'What?' Helen looked at her, startled.

'Gor blimey,' said Jane.

The colour slowly rose to Helen's pale cheeks.

'I suppose that's Andrew again.'

'He said you were under the impression that we'd spend our time stuffing wet lettuce leaves down each other's bosoms and keeping coal in the bath.'

'Garden gnomes.' Helen said it solemnly. 'That's what I was scared of.'

'*Garden gnomes?* Were you really?'

'Well – you know! Not seriously. But I did think you might do ghastly things to the house. I don't any more. I've seen the plans. I think your dad will make a really good job of it.'

'He will. He's got a thing about old houses.'

They went on for a few minutes in silence.

'Do you mind having to leave Shallaford?' said Jane.

'Yes, but there's no good crying over what can't

be helped and I feel better about it now that I've come to know you all. What about you?' Helen turned, solemnly, to look at Jane. 'Do you mind about leaving London?'

'Not as much as I did. I guess you can get used to anything.'

'I'm really glad you've come to Martello. I was dreading coming here on my own.'

'Why did you come here?' That was still one of the puzzles to Jane, Helen leaving her posh boarding school to go comprehensive. 'It's probably very vulgar of me to ask – very wet lettuce leaf-ish – but couldn't you afford to go on paying fees any more?'

'Oh, yes! We're not as broke as all that – especially now your parents are buying the house. It was my own choice.' Helen said it defiantly. 'I wanted to come here.'

'Even though you were dreading it?'

'Yes; I wanted a change. I wanted to enter the real world – see what it was like for other people. I've lived in cloud cuckooland all my life. Even when we were broke it wasn't broke like real people are broke. People that can't pay the mortgage, or haven't got a roof over their heads. All it meant for us was not having the money to repair the roof. It all seemed such a – such a sham. And anyway,' said Helen. 'I couldn't do the A levels I wanted at my other place.'

'That, of course, is the real reason!' said Jane; but Helen hadn't yet reached the stage where she could be teased.

This, after almost a term at their new school, was the first really intimate conversation that they had had. Even on that terrible day when they had locked Andrew into the turret room and fled to the

148

telephone to call the police, they hadn't talked as they were talking now. Jane had been too shocked, Helen too awkward to do more than ask her if she were all right – if she wanted a cup of tea, if she wanted to lie down – and all the time the sound of Andrew's voice raging dementedly in their ears. And then at last the police had come, and had taken over, removing the necessity for conversation, and it had been a relief to both of them.

They would never achieve that same free and easy relationship that Jane had once enjoyed with Lynn, but she began to think that they might be friends. If it hadn't been for Helen, after all, Jane would almost certainly have ended up dead, smashed to pieces on the steps leading down to the Shallaford lawn. You owed a debt of gratitude, if nothing else, to the person who had saved your life.

'What made you come back that day?' Jane asked the question, curiously. She had often wondered. 'Was it just luck?'

'No.' Helen shook her head. 'I was worried about you being on your own. I'd – been to see Toby just the day before. All the things that kept happening to you . . . it brought it all back. Toby and – everything. Everything that had happened. I – I suddenly started wondering whether Andrew – whether he could possibly – whether he was really *capable*—' She stopped.

'I just didn't trust him any more. When he said he was going to see friends in Brighton . . . as far as I knew, he didn't have any friends in Brighton. So after he dropped me off I went round to the bus station and caught the first bus back. The only trouble was, it didn't leave for half an hour. I was really scared I might be too late . . . I kept torturing myself all the way, thinking I should have taken a cab.'

'What made you not trust him? Did you guess it was him doing all those things?'

'I – suspected. When you said a – a dead pigeon had come down the chimney and I – I couldn't think how it could have happened, because we'd had mesh put up there. And then your dad said he'd left it outside and I went to look and it was – it was Charlie! I thought at first one of the cats might have got him, but it wasn't a cat, his neck had been broken. And I knew then, I just knew, that it had to be Andrew. That bird was so tame, he'd let you do anything with him. And Andrew—' She stopped. 'He has done that sort of thing in the past.'

'But if you knew that it was him—' Jane spoke carefully, striving to keep any possible hint of criticism out of her voice – 'why didn't you say anything?'

'What could I have said? Andrew's killed Charlie and stuffed him down Jane's chimney? Mum wouldn't have believed me. She wouldn't hear anything against Andrew. Ever since Toby's accident, he's been her blue-eyed boy. I think she needed him – more than she needed me. Toby was always her favourite. I was never anything but second best; not with Mum. Andrew was a sort of . . . substitute. He could do anything he wanted with her. He had her wrapped right round his little finger. The only thing he couldn't stop her doing was selling the house, because there just wasn't any way she could have kept it on.'

'So he decided to take matters into his own hands and try and frighten us off.'

'I thought he was just . . . messing about. Up to his old tricks. He always used to enjoy scaring us, me and Toby, when we were little. He used to come down for holidays; we always hated it. He was the sort of boy that used to pull the legs off spiders, just for fun. I remember once he caught a mouse and wanted to barbecue it while it was still alive. He was really sadistic like that.'

'Is that why you wouldn't let the dogs go with us that time?'

'I was rude, wasn't I? I'm sorry about that, but I was really upset. I'd just discovered Charlie and – I had these visions of him doing something to the dogs.'

'Instead—' Jane attempted to make light of it – 'He did something to me! Or at any rate, tried to.'

'I never thought he'd go that far. Truly! Not until that last day, when Mum told me your parents were going to make an offer. Even then I – I didn't really believe he was that desperate. It was only when I got up there, on the roof, and I heard the things he was saying to you . . . I just ran and grabbed the gun and prayed I was going to be in time.'

'And then there was that awful telephone call,' said Jane. 'The one you said came from Lynn. Did you really think it was Lynn?'

'I wasn't sure. It sounded like her, but – there was just something about it . . . something – not quite right. That's why I listened in. You knew I listened in, didn't you? You nearly caught me at it.'

'I thought it was you making the call,' said Jane. 'Me? You thought it was *me*?'

'Well, it could have been. You could have pretended it was coming from outside . . . I wouldn't have known the difference.'

'It never occurred to me. I suppose I should have said something to you at the time.'

'I probably wouldn't have believed you,' said Jane. 'I was convinced it was you that was at the bottom of everything.'

'Yes, because of the radio that first night. Everyone thought it was me. Mum even told me off about it.'

'What I don't understand,' said Jane, 'is why *he* kept trying to convince me. Why he kept telling me all these things, like how unbalanced you were and how you couldn't bear the thought of the house being sold and how you were such a terrible snob . . . projecting it all on to you when really and truly he was just talking about himself.'

'He probably enjoyed it,' said Helen. 'It probably gave him a secret thrill. I shouldn't be surprised if deep down he hates me. I think he used to hate both of us now I look back on it. Me and Toby. I expect it was partly our own fault.'

Helen kicked at a stone that was on the path. They watched it roll away into the bushes that bordered the field.

'I never thought about it until now . . . we always used to try and run away from him and do things without him. I suppose he felt excluded, but there was just something so . . . creepy about him.'

Jane blushed. She hadn't thought that Andrew was creepy. There had been a time when she had thought she might almost be going to fall for him.

'He could be very charming,' she muttered.

'That's what made him so dangerous. He charmed

Mum so that she didn't know whether she was coming or going.'

I obviously have very bad taste in men, thought Jane, ruefully. It would be a long time before she trusted another one, she knew that.

'What will happen to him, do you think?'

'I suppose—' Helen said it gravely – 'I suppose he'll be kept where he is. Locked away.'

'So he'll be the one in an institution.'

'He deserves it! Don't go wasting any sympathy on him!'

'I can't help it,' whispered Jane. 'It seems so terrible.'

'What he tried to do to you was terrible! What he probably did to Toby was terrible!'

'I know, but – he's still so young!' So young, so beautiful . . . 'And he was going to go to university.'

'Is that what he told you?'

'Well – yes.' Jane faltered. 'Isn't it true?'

'It's just another of his stories. How could he be going to university when he never sat a single exam? Not even GCSEs. He was never at anywhere for long enough – they all kept chucking him out. I suppose in a way he did have a rotten sort of life. He used to love coming to Shallaford; it was the only real home he ever had. Not that Toby and I ever thought of it as his home, but he did. He used to tell us. He used to say, I'm going to live here one day. I remember once when we were little and they came to take him away – his mum and her latest boyfriend – he didn't want to go with them. He tried to shut himself in the turret room. He always used to hide in there. In the end they had to drag him out, and

153

he was screaming all the way down to the car: don't take me, don't take me! I don't want to go!'

'Don't!' Jane clapped her hands to her ears. 'It's dreadful!'

'But it isn't any excuse!'

'Except that when you know what people have been through . . . you begin to understand. You can almost even begin to feel sorry for them.'

'How can you say that?' Helen turned on her, wide-eyed; almost accusatory. 'After he tried to kill you?'

'I know he tried to kill me. But I still can feel sorry for him.'

Helen was silent a moment.

'I suppose I can too,' she said. 'In a way. When I think back. I can see now that he was badly treated. I can see that he was always unhappy. I can even see why he did what he did to you. Even why he – why he might have done that other thing. It's ghastly and it's twisted, but you're right: I can understand. I can see how things led up to it and how his mind got poisoned. But why did he have to go and kill Charlie? Why did he torture that mouse that time? There isn't any logic to that, not even twisted logic. They weren't doing him any harm – they weren't standing in his way. It was just sheer wanton cruelty, and when I think of that I hate him!'

'Yes.' Jane nodded, soberly. 'I could hate him for that. I hate anyone that ill-treats animals.'

'I suppose—' Helen said it hesitantly – 'I suppose someone like you probably thinks that I ill-treat animals, since I eat them.'

Jane said nothing. Once she would have waded

in, banners flying; but there were times when perhaps it was better to keep silent.

'Do you know, I really admire you for being a vegan? I do!' said Helen. 'I'm not even a vegetarian. I keep thinking that I ought to be, and then I'm just so weak I don't do anything about it.'

'Would you like me to nag at you?' said Jane.

'Yes! Why don't you? Keep on at me. Keep saying, Helen, that's a pig you're eating; Helen, that's a cow you're eating. That way, you'll get to my conscience.'

'Yes, and you'll get mad at me!'

'I won't,' said Helen. 'I promise.'

'I bet you will! People hate being nagged at.'

'Not if it's in a good cause.'

'Even though it's in a good cause.' Jane knew: she had tried it on her mum and dad. 'Still, I suppose if we're going to be friends—'

'I'd like to,' said Helen, shyly.

'In that case, no problem,' said Jane. She tucked her arm through Helen's. 'Friends don't mind being got mad at.'

THE END

ABOUT THE AUTHOR

Jean Ure had her first novel, *Dance for Two*, published while she was still at school and has been writing ever since. She studied at drama school, where she met her husband, and is now a full-time author of books for both young readers and adults, with more than fifty titles to her name. Her titles for Transworld include *One Green Leaf*, *The Other Side of the Fence*, *A Proper Little Nooryeff*, *You Win Some, You Lose Some* and *Dreaming of Larry* (all published by Corgi Freeway) and *A Place to Scream* (published by Doubleday).

A vegan and an animal rights worker, Jean lives in a 300-year-old house with her husband, five dogs and two cats.

DREAMING OF LARRY
Jean Ure

Judith is fifteen. With her strong
feminist principles, she's just not the
sort of girl to start 'going gooey'
over some boy.

Larry is older. Definitely upmarket, he's
the kind of sophisticated boy who can
make the silliest of her classmates go
weak at the knees.

Are they fated to be together? Judith
thinks so – especially when she finds
herself dreaming about Larry, and then
uncovers an intriguing link between
their two families in the past. But as
their light-hearted friendship begins to
develop into something much more
powerful, Judith faces a startling
confusion of new feelings – feelings
that she is not sure she is quite
ready to deal with . . .

'A delicious read' *Telegraph*

0 552 52615 0

A SELECTED LIST OF TITLES
AVAILABLE FROM CORGI FREEWAY BOOKS

☐ 52797 1	**A BONE FROM A DRY SEA**	*Peter Dickinson*	£2.99
☐ 52594 4	**DARKLING**	*K. M. Peyton*	£2.99
☐ 52406 9	**THE FAT GIRL**	*Marilyn Sachs*	£2.99
☐ 52506 5	**ONE GREEN LEAF**	*Jean Ure*	£2.25
☐ 52466 2	**THE OTHER SIDE OF THE FENCE**	*Jean Ure*	£2.99
☐ 52711 4	**A PROPER LITTLE NOORYEFF**	*Jean Ure*	£2.99
☐ 52431 X	**YOU WIN SOME, YOU LOSE SOME**	*Jean Ure*	£2.99
☐ 52615 0	**DREAMING OF LARRY**	*Jean Ure*	£2.99
☐ 52457 3	**PLEASE DON'T GO**	*Peggy Woodford*	£2.50
☐ 52744 2	**BLOOD AND MORTAR**	*Peggy Woodford*	£2.99